Ray Bradbury, one of the greatest writers of fantasy and horror fiction in the world today, has published some 500 short stories, novels, plays and poems since his first story appeared in *Weird Tales* when he was twenty years old. Among his many famous works are *Fahrenheit 451*, *The Illustrated Man* and *The Martian Chronicles*. He has also written the screenplays for *It Came from Outer Space*, *Something Wicked This Way Comes* and *Moby Dick*. Mr Bradbury was Idea Consultant for the United States Pavilion at the 1964 World's Fair, has written the basic scenario for the interior of Spaceship Earth at EPCOT, Disney World, and is doing consultant work on city engineering and rapid transit. When one of the Apollo Astronaut teams landed on the moon, they named Dandelion Crater there to honour Mr Bradbury's novel, *Dandelion Wine*.

By the same author

RAY BRADBURY

The Small Assassin

Grafton
An Imprint of HarperCollins*Publishers*

Grafton
An Imprint of HarperCollins*Publishers*
77–85 Fulham Palace Road,
Hammersmith, London W6 8JB

Published by Grafton 1976
9 8 7 6 5

'The Tombstone', 'The Smiling People', 'The Handler',
'Let's Play "Poison"', 'The Night' and 'The Dead Man' are
taken from *Dark Carnival*, first published in Great Britain by
Hamish Hamilton Ltd, 1948
'Jack-in-the-Box' is taken from *The October Country*, first
published in Great Britain by Rupert Hart-Davis Ltd, 1956
All other stories in this book appeared first in *Dark Carnival*
and were reprinted in *The October Country*

The Author asserts the moral right to
be identified as the author of this work

ISBN 0 586 04228 8

Set in Times

Printed in Great Britain by
HarperCollinsManufacturing Glasgow

To Grant M. Beach

Contents

The Small Assassin

Just when the idea occurred to her that she was being murdered she could not tell. There had been little subtle signs, little suspicions for the past month; things as deep as sea tides in her, like looking at a perfectly calm stretch of tropical water, wanting to bathe in it and finding, just as the tide takes your body, that monsters dwell just under the surface, things unseen, bloated, many-armed, sharp-finned, malignant and inescapable.

A room floated around her in an effluvium of hysteria. Sharp instruments hovered and there were voices, and people in sterile white masks.

My name, she thought, what is it?

Alice Leiber. It came to her. David Leiber's wife. But it gave her no comfort. She was alone with these silent, whispering white people and there was great pain and nausea and death-fear in her.

I am being murdered before their eyes. These doctors, these nurses don't realize what hidden thing has happened to me. David doesn't know. Nobody knows except me and – the killer, the little murderer, the small assassin.

I am dying and I can't tell them now. They'd laugh and call me one in delirium. They'll see the murderer and hold him and never think him responsible for my death. But here I am, in front of God and man, dying, no one to believe my story, everyone to doubt me, comfort me with lies, bury me in ignorance, mourn me and salvage my destroyer.

Where is David? she wondered. In the waiting room, smoking one cigarette after another, listening to the long tickings of the very slow clock?

Sweat exploded from all of her body at once, and with it

an agonized cry. Now. Now! Try and kill me, she screamed. Try, try, but I won't die! I won't!

There was a hollowness. A vacuum. Suddenly the pain fell away. Exhaustion, and dusk came around. It was over. Oh, God! She plummeted down and struck a black nothingness which gave way to nothingness and nothingness and another and still another . . .

Footsteps. Gentle, approaching footsteps.

Far away, a voice said, 'She's asleep. Don't disturb her.'

An odour of tweeds, a pipe, a certain shaving lotion. David was standing over her. And beyond him the immaculate smell of Dr Jeffers.

She did not open her eyes. 'I'm awake,' she said, quietly. It was a surprise, a relief to be able to speak, not to be dead.

'Alice,' someone said, and it was David beyond her closed eyes, holding her tired hands.

Would you like to meet the murderer, David? she thought. I hear your voice asking to see him, so there's nothing but for me to point him out to you.

David stood over her. She opened her eyes. The room came into focus. Moving a weak hand, she pulled aside a coverlet.

The murderer looked up at David Leiber with a small, red-faced, blue-eyed calm. Its eyes were deep and sparkling.

'Why!' cried David Leiber, smiling. 'He's a *fine* baby!'

Dr Jeffers was waiting for David Leiber the day he came to take his wife and new child home. He motioned Leiber to a chair in his office, gave him a cigar, lit one for himself, sat on the edge of his desk, puffing solemnly for a long moment. Then he cleared his throat, looked David Leiber straight on and said, 'Your wife doesn't like her child, Dave.'

'What!'

'It's been a hard thing for her. She'll need a lot of love this next year. I didn't say much at the time, but she was hysterical in the delivery room. The strange things she said – I won't repeat them. All I'll say is that she feels alien to the child. Now, this may simply be a thing we can clear up with one or two questions.' He sucked on his cigar another moment, then said, 'Is this child a "wanted" child, Dave?'

'Why do you ask?'

'It's vital.'

'Yes. Yes, it is a "wanted" child. We planned it together. Alice was so happy, a year ago, when –'

'Mmmm – That makes it more difficult. Because if the child was unplanned, it would be a simple case of a woman hating the idea of motherhood. That doesn't fit Alice.' Dr Jeffers took his cigar from his lips, rubbed his hand across his jaw. 'It must be something else, then. Perhaps something buried in her childhood that's coming out now. Or it might be the simple temporary doubt and distrust of any mother who's gone through the unusual pain and near-death that Alice has. If so, then a little time should heal that. I thought I'd tell you, though, Dave. It'll help you be easy and tolerant with her if she says anything about – well – about wishing the child had been born dead. And if things don't go well, the three of you drop in on me. I'm always glad to see old friends, eh? Here, take another cigar along for – ah – for the baby.'

It was a bright spring afternoon. Their car hummed along wide, tree-lined boulevards. Blue sky, flowers, a warm wind. Dave talked a lot, lit his cigar, talked some more. Alice answered directly, softly, relaxing a bit more as the trip progressed. But she held the baby not tightly or warmly or motherly enough to satisfy the queer ache in Dave's mind. She seemed to be merely carrying a porcelain figurine.

'Well,' he said, at last, smiling. 'What'll we name him?'

Alice Leiber watched green trees slide by. 'Let's not decide yet. I'd rather wait until we get an exceptional name for him. Don't blow smoke in his face.' Her sentences ran together with no change of tone. The last statement held no motherly reproof, no interest, no irritation. She just mouthed it and it was said.

The husband, disquieted, dropped the cigar from the window. 'Sorry,' he said.

The baby rested in the crook of his mother's arm, shadows of sun and tree changing his face. His blue eyes opened like fresh blue spring flowers. Moist noises came from the tiny, pink, elastic mouth.

Alice gave her baby a quick glance. Her husband felt her shiver against him.

'Cold?' he asked.

'A chill. Better raise the window, David.'

It was more than a chill. He rolled the window slowly up.

Suppertime.

Dave had brought the child from the nursery, propped him at a tiny, bewildered angle, supported by many pillows, in a newly purchased high chair.

Alice watched her knife and fork move. 'He's not high-chair size,' she said.

'Fun having him here, anyway,' said Dave, feeling fine. 'Everything's fun. At the office, too. Orders up to my nose. If I don't watch myself I'll make another fifteen thousand this year. Hey, look at Junior, will you? Drooling all down his chin!' He reached over to wipe the baby's mouth with his napkin. From the corner of his eye he realized that Alice wasn't even watching. He finished the job.

'I guess it wasn't very interesting,' he said, back again

at his food. 'But one would think a mother'd take some interest in her own child!'

Alice jerked her chin up. 'Don't speak that way! Not in front of him! Later, if you must.'

'Later?' he cried. 'In front of, in back of, what's the difference?' He quieted suddenly, swallowed, was sorry. 'All right. Okay. I know how it is.'

After dinner she let him carry the baby upstairs. She didn't tell him to; she *let* him.

Coming down, he found her standing by the radio, listening to music she didn't hear. Her eyes were closed, her whole attitude one of wondering, self-questioning. She started when he appeared.

Suddenly, she was at him, against him, soft, quick; the same. Her lips found him, kept him. He was stunned. Now that the baby was gone, upstairs, out of the room, she began to breathe again, live again. She was free. She was whispering, rapidly, endlessly.

'Thank you, thank you, darling. For being yourself, always. Dependable, so very dependable!'

He had to laugh. 'My father told me, "Son, provide for your family!"'

Wearily, she rested her dark, shining hair against his neck. 'You've overdone it. Sometimes I wish we were just the way we were when we were first married. No responsibilities, nothing but ourselves. No – no babies.'

She crushed his hand in hers, a supernatural whiteness in her face.

'Oh, Dave, once it was just you and me. We protected each other, and now we protect the baby, but get no protection from it. Do you understand? Lying in the hospital I had time to think a lot of things. The world is evil –'

'Is it?'

'Yes. It is. But laws protect us from it. And when there aren't laws, then love does the protecting. You're protected from my hurting you, by my love. You're vulnerable to me, of all people, but love shields you. I feel no fear of you, because love cushions all your irritations, unnatural instincts, hatreds and immaturities. But – what about the baby? It's too young to know love, or a law of love, or anything, until we teach it. And in the meantime be vulnerable to it.'

'Vulnerable to a baby?' He held her away and laughed gently.

'Does a baby know the difference between right and wrong?' she asked.

'No. But it'll learn.'

'But a baby is so new, so amoral, so conscience-free.' She stopped. Her arms dropped from him and she turned swiftly. 'That noise? What was it?'

Leiber looked around the room. 'I didn't hear –'

She stared at the library door. 'In there,' she said, slowly.

Leiber crossed the room, opened the door and switched the library lights on and off. 'Not a thing.' He came back to her. 'You're worn out. To bed with you – right now.'

Turning out the lights together, they walked slowly up the soundless hall stairs, not speaking. At the top she apologized. 'My wild talk, darling. Forgive me. I'm exhausted.'

He understood, and said so.

She paused, undecided, by the nursery door. Then she fingered the brass knob sharply, walked in. He watched her approach the crib much too carefully, look down, and stiffen as if she'd been struck in the face. 'David!'

Leiber stepped forward, reached the crib.

The baby's face was bright red and very moist; his small pink mouth opened and shut, opened and shut; his eyes were a fiery blue. His hands leapt about in the air.

'Oh,' said Dave, 'he's just been crying.'

'Has he?' Alice Leiber seized the crib-railing to balance herself. 'I didn't hear him.'

'The door was closed.'

'Is that why he breathes so hard, why his face is red?'

'Sure. Poor little guy. Crying all alone in the dark. He can sleep in our room tonight, just in case he cries.'

'You'll spoil him,' his wife said.

Leiber felt her eyes follow as he rolled the crib into their bedroom. He undressed silently, sat on the edge of the bed. Suddenly he lifted his head, swore under his breath, snapped his fingers. 'Damn it! Forgot to tell you. I must fly to Chicago Friday.'

'Oh, David.' Her voice was lost in the room.

'I've put this trip off for two months, and now it's so critical I just *have* to go.'

'I'm afraid to be alone.'

'We'll have the new cook by Friday. She'll be here all the time. I'll only be gone a few days.'

'I'm afraid. I don't know of what. You wouldn't believe me if I told you. I guess I'm crazy.'

He was in bed now. She darkened the room; he heard her walk around the bed, throw back the cover, slide in. He smelled the warm woman-smell of her next to him. He said, 'If you want me to wait a few days, perhaps I could –'

'No,' she said, unconvinced. 'You go. I know it's important. It's just that I keep thinking about what I told you. Laws and love and protection. Love protects you from me. But, the baby –' She took a breath. 'What protects you from him, David?'

Before he could answer, before he could tell her how silly it was, speaking of infants, she switched on the bed light, abruptly.

'Look,' she said, pointing.

The baby lay wide-awake in its crib, staring straight at him, with deep, sharp blue eyes.

The lights went out again. She trembled against him.

'It's not nice being afraid of the thing you birthed.' Her whisper lowered, became harsh, fierce, swift. 'He tried to kill me! He lies there, listens to us talking, waiting for you to go away so he can try to kill me again! I swear it!' Sobs broke from her.

'Please,' he kept saying, soothing her. 'Stop it, stop it. Please.'

She cried in the dark for a long time. Very late she relaxed, shakingly, against him. Her breathing came soft, warm, regular, her body twitched its worn reflexes and she slept.

He drowsed.

And just before his eyes lidded wearily down, sinking him into deeper and yet deeper tides, he heard a strange little sound of awareness and awakeness in the room.

The sound of small, moist, pinkly elastic lips.

The baby.

And then – sleep.

In the morning, the sun blazed. Alice smiled.

David Leiber dangled his watch over the crib. 'See, baby? Something bright. Something pretty. Sure. Sure. Something bright. Something pretty.'

Alice smiled. She told him to go ahead, fly to Chicago, she'd be very brave, no need to worry. She'd take care of baby. Oh, yes, she'd take care of him, all right.

The aeroplane went east. There was a lot of sky, a lot of sun and clouds and Chicago running over the horizon. Dave was dropped into the rush of ordering, planning, banqueting, telephoning, arguing in conference. But he wrote letters each day and sent telegrams to Alice and the baby.

On the evening of his sixth day away from home he received the long-distance phone call. Los Angeles.

'Alice?'

'No, Dave. This is Jeffers speaking.'

'Doctor!'

'Hold on to yourself, son. Alice is sick. You'd better get the next plane home. It's pneumonia. I'll do everything I can, boy. If only it wasn't so soon after the baby. She needs strength.'

Leiber dropped the phone into its cradle. He got up, with no feet under him, and no hands and no body. The hotel room blurred and fell apart.

'Alice,' he said, blindly, starting for the door.

The propellers spun about, whirled, fluttered, stopped; time and space were put behind. Under his hand, David felt the doorknob turn; under his feet the floor assumed reality, around him flowed the walls of a bedroom, and in the late-afternoon sunlight Dr Jeffers stood, turning from a window, as Alice lay waiting in her bed, something carved from a fall of winter snow. Then Dr Jeffers was talking, talking continuously, gently, the sound rising and falling through the lamplight, a soft flutter, a white murmur of voice.

'Your wife's too good a mother, Dave. She worried more about the baby than herself . . .'

Somewhere in the paleness of Alice's face, there was a sudden constriction which smoothed itself out before it was realized. Then, slowly, half-smiling, she began to talk and she talked as a mother should about this, that and the other thing, the telling detail, the minute-by-minute and hour-by-hour report of a mother concerned with a dollhouse world and the miniature life of that world. But she could not stop; the spring was wound tight, and her voice rushed on to anger, fear and the faintest touch of revulsion, which did not change Dr Jeffers' expression, but caused Dave's heart to match the rhythm of this talk that quickened and could not stop:

'The baby wouldn't sleep. I thought he was sick. He just

lay, staring, in his crib, and late at night he'd cry. So loud, he'd cry, and he'd cry all night and all night. I couldn't quiet him, and I couldn't rest.'

Dr Jeffers' head nodded slowly, slowly. 'Tired herself right into pneumonia. But she's full of sulpha now and on the safe side of the whole damn thing.'

David felt ill. 'The baby, what about the baby?'

'Fit as a fiddle; cock of the walk!'

'Thanks, Doctor.'

The doctor walked off away and down the stairs, opened the front door faintly, and was gone.

'David!'

He turned to her frightened whisper.

'It was the baby again.' She clutched his hand. 'I try to lie to myself and say that I'm a fool, but the baby knew I was weak from the hospital, so he cried all night every night, and when he wasn't crying he'd be much too quiet. I knew if I switched on the light he'd be there, staring up at me.'

David felt his body close in on itself like a fist. He remembered seeing the baby, feeling the baby, awake in the dark, awake very late at night when babies should be asleep. Awake and lying there, silent as thought, not crying, but watching from its crib. He thrust the thought aside. It was insane.

Alice went on. 'I was going to kill the baby. Yes, I was. When you'd been gone only a day on your trip I went to his room and put my hands about his neck; and I stood there, for a long time, thinking, afraid. Then I put the covers up over his face and turned him over on his face and pressed him down and left him that way and ran out of the room.'

He tried to stop her.

'No, let me finish,' she said, hoarsely, looking at the wall. 'When I left his room I thought, It's simple. Babies smother every day. No one'll ever know. But when I came back to see him dead, David, he was alive! Yes, alive, turned over on his back, alive and smiling and breathing. And I couldn't touch him again after that. I left him there and I didn't come back, not to feed him or look at him or do anything. Perhaps the cook tended to him. I don't know. All I know is that his crying kept me awake, and I thought all through the night, and walked around the rooms and now I'm sick.' She was almost finished now. 'The baby lies there and thinks of ways to kill me. Simple ways. Because he knows I know so much about him. I have no love for him; there is no protection between us; there never will be.'

She was through. She collapsed inward on herself and finally slept. David Leiber stood for a long time over her, not able to move. His blood was frozen in his body, not a cell stirred anywhere, anywhere at all.

The next morning there was only one thing to do. He did it. He walked into Dr Jeffers' office and told him the whole thing, and listened to Jeffers' tolerant replies:

'Let's take this thing slowly, son. It's quite natural for mothers to hate their children, sometimes. We have a label for it – ambivalence. The ability to hate, while loving. Lovers hate each other, frequently. Children detest their mothers –'

Leiber interrupted. 'I never hated my mother.'

'You won't admit it, naturally. People don't enjoy admitting hatred for their loved ones.'

'So Alice hates her baby.'

'Better say she has an obsession. She's gone a step further than plain, ordinary ambivalence. A Caesarian operation brought the child into the world and almost took Alice out of it. She blames the child for her near-death and her pneumonia. She's projecting her troubles, blaming them on the handiest object she can use as a source of blame. We *all* do it. We stumble into a chair and curse the furniture, not our own clumsiness. We miss a golf-stroke and damn the turf or our club, or the make of ball. If our business fails we blame the gods, the weather, our luck. All I can tell you is what I told you before. Love her. Finest medicine in the world. Find little ways of showing your affection, give her security. Find ways of showing her how harmless and innocent the child is. Make her feel that the baby was worth the risk. After a while, she'll settle down, forget about death, and begin to love the child. If she doesn't come around in the next month or so, ask me. I'll recommend a good psychiatrist. Go on along now, and take that look off your face.'

When summer came, things seemed to settle, become easier. Dave worked, immersed himself in office detail, but found much time for his wife. She, in turn, took long walks, gained strength, played an occasional light game of badminton. She rarely burst out any more. She seemed to have rid herself of her fears.

Except on one certain midnight when a sudden summer wind swept around the house, warm and swift, shaking the trees like so many shining tambourines. Alice wakened, trembling, and slid over into her husband's arms, and let him console her, and ask her what was wrong.

She said, 'Something's here in the room, watching us.'

He switched on the light. 'Dreaming again,' he said. 'You're better, though. Haven't been troubled for a long time.'

She sighed as he clicked off the light again, and suddenly she slept. He held her, considering what a sweet, weird creature she was, for about half an hour.

He heard the bedroom door sway open a few inches.

There was nobody at the door. No reason for it to come open. The wind had died.

He waited. It seemed like an hour he lay silently, in the dark.

Then, far away, wailing like some small meteor dying in the vast inky gulf of space, the baby began to cry in his nursery.

It was a small, lonely sound in the middle of the stars and the dark and the breathing of this woman in his arms and the wind beginning to sweep through the trees again.

Leiber counted to one hundred, slowly. The crying continued.

Carefully disengaging Alice's arm he slipped from bed, put on his slippers, robe, and moved quietly from the room.

He'd go downstairs, he thought, fix some warm milk, bring it up, and –

The blackness dropped out from under him. His foot slipped and plunged. Slipped on something soft. Plunged into nothingness.

He thrust his hands out, caught frantically at the railing. His body stopped falling. He held. He cursed.

The 'something soft' that had caused his feet to slip, rustled and thumped down a few steps. His head rang. His heart hammered at the base of his throat, thick and shot with pain.

Why do careless people leave things strewn about a house? He groped carefully with his fingers for the object that had almost spilled him headlong down the stairs.

His hand froze, startled. His breath went in. His heart held one or two beats.

The thing he held in his hand was a toy. A large cumbersome, patchwork doll he had bought as a joke, for –

For the baby.

Alice drove him to work the next day.

She slowed the car half way downtown; pulled to the kerb and stopped it. Then she turned on the seat and looked at her husband.

'I want to go away on a vacation. I don't know if you

can make it now, darling, but if not, please let me go alone. We can get someone to take care of the baby, I'm sure. But I just have to get away. I thought I was growing out of this – this *feeling*. But I haven't. I can't stand being in the room with him. He looks up at me as if he hates me, too. I can't put my finger on it; all I know is I want to get away before something happens.'

He got out on his side of the car, came around, motioned to her to move over, got in. 'The only thing you're going to do is see a good psychiatrist. And if he suggests a vacation, well, okay. But this can't go on; my stomach's in knots all the time.' He started the car. 'I'll drive the rest of the way.'

Her head was down; she was trying to keep back tears. She looked up when they reached his office building. 'All right. Make the appointment. I'll go talk to anyone you want, David.'

He kissed her. 'Now, you're talking sense, lady. Think you can drive home okay?'

'Of course, silly.'

'See you at supper, then. Drive carefully.'

'Don't I always? Bye.'

He stood on the kerb, watching her drive off, the wind taking hold of her long, dark, shining hair. Upstairs, a minute later, he phoned Jeffers and arranged an appointment with a reliable neuropsychiatrist.

The day's work went uneasily. Things fogged over; and in the fog he kept seeing Alice lost and calling his name. So much of her fear had come over to him. She actually had him convinced that the child was in some ways not quite natural.

He dictated long, uninspired letters. He checked some shipments downstairs. Assistants had to be questioned, and kept going. At the end of the day he was exhausted, his head throbbed, and he was very glad to go home.

On the way down in the elevator he wondered, What if

I told Alice about the toy – that patchwork doll – I slipped on on the stairs last night? Lord, wouldn't *that* back her off? No, I won't ever tell her. Accidents are, after all, accidents.

Daylight lingered in the sky as he drove home in a taxi. In front of the house he paid the driver and walked slowly up the cement walk, enjoying the light that was still in the sky and the trees. The white colonial front of the house looked unnaturally silent and uninhabited, and then, quietly, he remembered this was Thursday, and the hired help they were able to obtain from time to time were all gone for the day.

He took a deep breath of air. A bird sang behind the house. Traffic moved on the boulevard a block away. He twisted the key in the door. The knob turned under his fingers, oiled, silent.

The door opened. He stepped in, put his hat on the chair with his briefcase, started to shrug out of his coat, when he looked up.

Late sunlight streamed down the stairwell from the window near the top of the hall. Where the sunlight touched it took on the bright colour of the patchwork doll sprawled at the bottom of the stairs.

But he paid no attention to the toy.

He could only look, and not move, and look again at Alice.

Alice lay in a broken, grotesque, pallid gesturing and angling of her thin body, at the bottom of the stairs, like a crumpled doll that doesn't want to play any more, ever.

Alice was dead.

The house remained quiet, except for the sound of his heart.

She was dead.

He held her head in his hands, he felt her fingers. He held her body. But she wouldn't live. She wouldn't even try to live. He said her name, out loud, many times, and he tried, once again, by holding her to him, to give her back some of the warmth she had lost, but that didn't help.

He stood up. He must have made a phone call. He didn't remember. He found himself, suddenly, upstairs. He opened the nursery door and walked inside and stared blankly at the crib. His stomach was sick. He couldn't see very well.

The baby's eyes were closed, but his face was red, moist with perspiration, as if he'd been crying long and hard.

'She's dead,' said Leiber to the baby. 'She's dead.'

Then he started laughing low and soft and continuously for a long time until Dr Jeffers walked in out of the night and slapped him again and again across his face.

'Snap out of it! Pull yourself together!'

'She fell down the stairs, Doctor. She tripped on a patchwork doll and fell. I almost slipped on it the other night, myself. And now –'

The doctor shook him.

'Doc, Doc, Doc,' said Dave, hazily. 'Funny thing. Funny. I – I finally thought of a name for the baby.'

The doctor said nothing.

Leiber put his head back in his trembling hands and spoke the words. 'I'm going to have him christened next Sunday. Know what name I'm giving him? I'm going to call him Lucifer.'

It was eleven at night. A lot of strange people had come and gone through the house, taking the essential flame with them – Alice.

David Leiber sat across from the doctor in the library.

'Alice wasn't crazy,' he said, slowly. 'She had good reason to fear the baby.'

Jeffers exhaled. 'Don't follow after her! She blamed the child for her sickness, now you blame it for her death. She stumbled on a toy, remember that. You can't blame the child.'

'You mean Lucifer?'

'Stop calling him that!'

Leiber shook his head. 'Alice heard things at night, moving in the hall. You want to know what made those noises, Doctor? They were made by the baby. Four months old, moving in the dark, listening to us talk. Listening to every word!' He held to the sides of the chair. 'And if I turned the lights on, a baby is so small. It can hide behind furniture, a door, against a wall – below eye-level.'

'I want you to stop this!' said Jeffers.

'Let me say what I think or I'll go crazy. When I went to Chicago, who was it kept Alice awake, tiring her into pneumonia? The baby! And when Alice didn't die, then he tried killing me. It was simple; leave a toy on the stairs, cry in the night until your father goes downstairs to fetch your milk, and stumbles. A crude trick, but effective. It didn't get me. But it killed Alice dead.'

David Leiber stopped long enough to light a cigarette. 'I should have caught on. I'd turn on the lights in the middle of the night, many nights, and the baby'd be lying there, eyes wide. Most babies sleep all the time. Not this one. He stayed awake, thinking.'

'Babies don't think.'

'He stayed awake doing whatever he *could* do with his brain, then. What in hell do we know about a baby's mind? He had every reason to hate Alice; she suspected him for what he was – certainly not a normal child. Something – different. What do you know of babies, Doctor? The general run, yes. You know, of course, how babies kill their mothers at birth. Why? Could it be resentment at being forced into a lousy world like this one?'

Leiber leaned towards the doctor, tiredly. 'It all ties up. Suppose that a few babies out of all the millions born are instantaneously able to move, see, hear, think, like many animals and insects can. Insects are born self-sufficient. In a few weeks most mammals and birds adjust. But children take years to speak and learn to stumble around on their weak legs.

'But suppose one child in a billion is – strange? Born perfectly aware, able to think, instinctively. Wouldn't it be a perfect set-up, a perfect blind for anything the baby might want to do? He could pretend to be ordinary, weak, crying, ignorant. With just a *little* expenditure of energy he could crawl about a darkened house, listening. And how easy to place obstacles at the top of stairs. How easy to cry all night and tire a mother into pneumonia. How easy, right at birth, to be so close to the mother that *a few deft manoeuvres might cause peritonitis!*'

'For God's sake!' Jeffers was on his feet. 'That's a repulsive thing to say!'

'It's a repulsive thing I'm speaking of. How many mothers have died at the birth of their children? How many have suckled strange little improbabilities who cause death one way or another? Strange, red little creatures with brains that work in a bloody darkness we can't even guess at. Elemental little brains, aswarm with racial memory, hatred, a raw cruelty, with no more thought than self-preservation. And self-preservation in this case consisted of eliminating a mother who realized what a horror she had birthed. I ask you, Doctor, what is there in the world more selfish than a baby? Nothing!'

Jeffers scowled and shook his head, helplessly.

Leiber dropped his cigarette down. 'I'm not claiming any great strength for the child. Just enough to crawl around a little, a few months ahead of schedule. Just enough to listen all the time. Just enough to cry late at night. That's enough, more than enough.'

Jeffers tried ridicule. 'Call it murder, then. But murder must be motivated. What motive had the child?'

Leiber was ready with the answer. 'What is more at peace, more dreamfully content, at ease, at rest, fed, comforted, unbothered, than an unborn child? Nothing. It floats in a sleepy, timeless wonder of nourishment and silence. Then, suddenly, it is asked to give up its berth, is forced to vacate, rushed out into a noisy, uncaring, selfish world where it is asked to shift for itself, to hunt, to feed from the hunting, to seek after a vanishing love that once was its unquestionable right, to meet confusion instead of inner silence and conservative slumber! And the child *resents* it! Resents the cold air, the huge spaces, the sudden departure from familiar things. And in the tiny filament of brain the only thing the child knows is selfishness and hatred because the spell has been rudely shattered. Who is responsible for this disenchantment, this rude breaking of the spell? The mother. So here the new child has someone to hate with all its unreasoning mind. The mother has cast it out, rejected it. And the father is no better, kill him, too! He's responsible in *his* way!'

Jeffers interrupted: 'If what you say is true, then every woman in the world would have to look on her baby as something to dread, something to wonder about.'

'And why not? Hasn't the child a perfect alibi? A thousand years of accepted medical belief protects him. By all natural accounts he is helpless, not responsible. The child is born hating. And things grow worse, instead of better. At first the baby gets a certain amount of attention and mothering. But then as time passes, things change. When very new, a baby has the power to make parents do silly things when it cries or sneezes, jump when it makes a noise. As the years pass, the baby feels even that small power slip rapidly, for ever away, never to return. Why shouldn't it grasp all the power it can have? Why shouldn't it jockey for position while it has all the advantages? In later years it would be too late to express its hatred. *Now* would be the time to strike.'

Leiber's voice was very soft, very low.

'My little boy baby, lying in his crib nights, his face

moist and red and out of breath. From crying? No. From climbing slowly out of his crib, from crawling long distances through darkened hallways. My little boy baby. I want to kill him.'

The doctor handed him a water glass and some pills. 'You're not killing anyone. You're going to sleep for twenty-four hours. Sleep'll change your mind. Take this.'

Leiber drank down the pills and let himself be led upstairs to his bedroom, crying, and felt himself being put to bed. The doctor waited until he was moving deep into sleep, then left the house.

Leiber, alone, drifted down, down.

He heard a noise. 'What's – what's *that*?' he demanded, feebly.

Something moved in the hall.

David Leiber slept.

Very early the next morning, Dr Jeffers drove up to the house. It was a good morning, and he was here to drive Leiber to the country for a rest. Leiber would still be asleep upstairs. Jeffers had given him enough sedative to knock him out for at least fifteen hours.

He rang the doorbell. No answer. The servants were probably not up. Jeffers tried the front door, found it open, stepped in. He put his medical kit on the nearest chair.

Something white moved out of sight at the top of the stairs. Just a suggestion of a movement. Jeffers hardly noticed it.

The smell of gas was in the house.

Jeffers ran upstairs, crashed into Leiber's bedroom.

Leiber lay motionless on the bed, and the room billowed with gas, which hissed from a released jet at the base of the wall near the door. Jeffers twisted it off, then forced up all the windows and ran back to Leiber's body.

The body was cold. It had been dead quite a few hours.

Coughing violently, the doctor hurried from the room, eyes watering. Leiber hadn't turned on the gas himself. He *couldn't* have. Those sedatives had knocked him out, he wouldn't have wakened until noon. It wasn't suicide. Or was there the faintest possibility?

Jeffers stood in the hall for five minutes. Then he walked to the door of the nursery. It was shut. He opened it. He walked inside and to the crib.

The crib was empty.

He stood swaying by the crib for half a minute, then he said something to nobody in particular.

'The nursery door blew shut. You couldn't get back into your crib where it was safe. You didn't plan on the door blowing shut. A little thing like a slammed door can ruin the best of plans. I'll find you somewhere in the house, hiding, pretending to be something you are not.' The doctor looked dazed. He put his hand to his head and smiled palely. 'Now I'm talking like Alice and David talked. But, I can't take any chances. I'm not sure of anything, but I can't take any chances.'

He walked downstairs, opened his medical bag on the chair, took something out of it and held it in his hands.

Something rustled down the hall. Something very small and very quiet. Jeffers turned rapidly.

I had to operate to bring you into this world, he thought. Now I guess I can operate to take you out of it . . .

He took half-a-dozen slow, sure steps forward into the hall. He raised his hand into the sunlight.

'See, baby! Something bright – something pretty!'

A scalpel.

The Next in Line

It was a little caricature of a town square. In it were the following fresh ingredients: a candy-box of a bandstand where men stood on Thursday and Sunday nights exploding music; fine, green-patinated bronze-copper benches all scrolled and flourished; fine blue and pink tiled walks – blue as women's newly lacquered eyes, pink as women's hidden wonders; and fine French-clipped trees in the shapes of exact hatboxes. The whole, from your hotel window, had the fresh ingratiation and unbelievable fantasy one might expect of a French villa in the nineties. But no, this was Mexico! and this a plaza in a small colonial Mexican town, with a fine State Opera House (in which movies were shown for two pesos admission: *Rasputin and the Empress, The Big House, Madame Curie, Love Affair, Mama Loves Papa*).

Joseph came out on the sun-heated balcony in the morning and knelt by the grille, pointing his little box Brownie. Behind him, in the bath, the water was running and Marie's voice came out:

'What're you doing?'

He muttered '– a picture.' She asked again. He clicked the shutter, stood up, wound the spool inside, squinting, and said, 'Took a picture of the town square. God, didn't those men shout last night? I didn't sleep until two-thirty. We would have to arrive when the local Rotary's having its whinging.'

'What're our plans for today?' she asked.

'We're going to see the mummies,' he said.

'Oh,' she said. There was a long silence.

He came in, set the camera down, and lit himself a cigarette.

'I'll go up and see them alone,' he said, 'if you'd rather.'

'No,' she said, not very loud. 'I'll go along. But I wish we could forget the whole thing. It's such a lovely little town.'

'Look here!' he cried, catching a movement from the corner of his eyes. He hurried to the balcony, stood there, his cigarette smoking and forgotten in his fingers. 'Come quick, Marie!'

'I'm drying myself,' she said.

'Please, hurry,' he said, fascinated, looking down into the street.

There was movement behind him, and then the odour of soap and water-rinsed flesh, wet towel, fresh cologne; Marie was at his elbow. 'Stay right there,' she cautioned him, 'so I can look without exposing myself. I'm stark. What *is* it?'

'Look!' he cried.

A procession travelled along the street. One man led it, with a package on his head. Behind him came women in black rebozos, chewing away the peels of oranges and spitting them on the cobbles; little children at their elbows, men ahead of them. Some ate sugar-cane, gnawing away at the outer bark until it split down and they pulled it off in great hunks to get at the succulent pulp, and the juicy sinews on which to suck. In all, there were fifty people.

'Joe,' said Marie behind him, holding his arm.

It was no ordinary package the first man in the procession carried on his head, balanced delicately as a chicken-plume. It was covered with silver satin and silver fringe and silver rosettes. And he held it gently with one brown hand, the other hand swinging free.

This was a funeral and the little package was a coffin.

Joseph glanced at his wife.

She was the colour of fine, fresh milk. The pink colour of the bath was gone. Her heart had sucked it all down to some hidden vacuum in her. She held fast to the french doorway and watched the travelling people go, watched them eat fruit, heard them talk gently, laugh gently. She forgot she was naked.

He said, 'Some little girl or boy gone to a happier place.'

'Where are they taking – her?'

She did not think it unusual, her choice of the feminine pronoun. Already she had identified herself with that tiny fragment parcelled like an unripe variety of fruit. Now, in this moment, she was being carried up the hill within compressing darkness, a stone in a peach, silent and terrified, the touch of the father against the coffin material outside; gentle and noiseless and firm inside.

'To the graveyard, naturally; that's where they're taking her,' he said, the cigarette making a filter of smoke across his casual face.

'Not *the* graveyard?'

'There's only one cemetery in these towns, you know that. They usually hurry it. That little girl had probably been dead only a few hours.'

'A few hours –'

She turned away, quite ridiculous, quite naked, with only the towel supported by her limp, untrying hands. She walked towards the bed. 'A few hours ago she was alive, and now –'

He went on, 'Now they're hurrying her up the hill. The climate isn't kind to the dead. It's hot, there's no embalming. They have to finish it quickly.'

'But to *that* graveyard, that horrible place,' she said, with a voice from a dream.

'Oh, the mummies,' he said. 'Don't let that bother you.'

She sat on the bed, again and again stroking the towel laid across her lap. Her eyes were blind as the brown paps of her breasts. She did not see him or the room. She knew that if he snapped his fingers or coughed, she wouldn't even look up.

'They were eating fruit at her funeral, and laughing,' she said.

'It's a long climb to the cemetery.'

She shuddered, a convulsive motion, like a fish trying to free itself from a deep-swallowed hook. She lay back and he looked at her as one examines a poor sculpture; all criticism, all quiet and easy and uncaring. She wondered idly just how much his hands had had to do with the broadening and flattening and changement of her body. Certainly this was not the body he'd started with. It was past saving now. Like clay which the sculptor has carelessly impregnated with water, it was impossible to shape again. In order to shape clay you warm it with your hands, evaporate the moisture with heat. But there was no more of that fine summer weather between them. There was no warmth to bake away the ageing moisture that collected and made pendant now her breasts and body. When the heat is gone, it is marvellous and unsettling to see how quickly a vessel stores self-destroying water in its cells.

'I don't feel well,' she said. She lay there, thinking it over. 'I don't feel well,' she said again, when he made no response. After another minute or two she lifted herself. 'Let's not stay here another night, Joe.'

'But it's a wonderful town.'

'Yes, but we've seen everything.' She got up. She knew what came next. Gayness, blitheness, encouragement, everything quite false and hopeful. 'We could go on to Patzcuaro. Make it in no time. You won't have to pack, I'll do it all myself, darling! We can get a room at the Don Posada there. They say it's a beautiful little town –'

'This,' he remarked, 'is a beautiful little town.'

'Bougainvillaea climb all over the buildings –' she said.

'These' – he pointed to some flowers at the window – 'are bougainvillaea.'

'– and we'd fish, you like fishing,' she said in bright haste. 'And I'd fish, too, I'd learn, yes I would, I've always *wanted* to learn! And they say the Tarascan Indians there are almost Mongoloid in feature, and don't speak much Spanish, and from there we could go to Paracutin, that's near Uruapan, and they have some of the finest lacquered boxes there, oh, it'll be fun Joe, I'll pack. You just take it easy, and –'

'Marie.'

He stopped her with one word as she ran to the bathroom door.

'Yes?'

'I thought you said you didn't feel well?'

'I didn't. I don't. But, thinking of all those swell places –'

'We haven't seen one-tenth of this town,' he explained logically. 'There's that statue of Morelos on the hill, I want a shot of that, and some of that French architecture up the street . . . we've travelled three hundred miles and we've been here one day and now you want to rush off somewhere else. I've already paid the rent for another night . . .'

'You can get it back,' she said.

'Why do you want to run away?' he said, looking at her with an attentive simplicity. 'Don't you like the town?'

'I simply adore it,' she said, her cheeks white, smiling. 'It's so green and pretty.'

'Well, then,' he said. 'Another day. You'll love it. That's settled.'

She started to speak.

'Yes?' he asked.

'Nothing.'

She closed the bathroom door. Behind it she rattled open a medicine box. Water rushed into a tumbler. She was taking something for her stomach.

He came to the bathroom door.

'Marie, the mummies don't bother you, do they?'

'Unh-unh,' she said.

'Was it the funeral, then?'

'Unh.'

'Because, if you were really afraid, I'd pack in a moment, you know that, darling.'

He waited.

'No, I'm not afraid,' she said.

'Good girl,' he said.

The graveyard was enclosed by a thick adobe wall, and at its four corners small stone angels tilted out on stony wings, their grimy heads capped with bird droppings, their hands gifted with amulets of the same substance, their faces unquestionably freckled.

In the warm smooth flow of sunlight which was like a depthless, tideless river, Joseph and Marie climbed up the hill, their shadows slanting blue behind them. Helping one another, they made the cemetery gate, swung back the Spanish blue iron grille and entered.

It was several mornings after the celebratory fiesta of El Día de Muerte, the Day of the Dead, and ribbons and ravels of tissue and sparkle-tape still clung like insane hair to the raised stones, to the hand-carved, love-polished crucifixes, and to the above-ground tombs which resembled marble jewel-cases. There were statues frozen in angelic postures over gravel mounds, and intricately carved stones tall as men with angels spilling all down their rims, and tombs as big and ridiculous as beds put out to dry in the sun after some nocturnal accident. And within the four walls of the yard, inserted into square mouths and slots, were coffins, walled in, plated in by marble plates and plaster, upon which names were struck and upon which hung tin pictures, cheap peso portraits of the inserted dead. Thumb-tacked to the different pictures were trinkets they'd loved in life, silver charms, silver arms, legs, bodies, silver cups, silver dogs, silver church medallions, bits of

red crêpe and blue ribbon. On some places were painted
slats of tin showing the dead rising to heaven in oil-tinted
angels' arms.

Looking at the graves again, they saw the remnants of
the death fiesta. The little tablets of tallow splashed over
the stones by the lighted festive candles, the wilted orchid
blossoms lying like crushed red-purple tarantulas against
the milky stones, some of them looking horridly sexual,
limp and withered. There were loop-frames of cactus
leaves, bamboo, reeds, and wild, dead morning-glories.
There were circles of gardenias and sprigs of bougainvillaea, desiccated. The entire floor of the yard seemed a
ballroom after a wild dancing, from which the participants
have fled; the tables askew, confetti, candles, ribbons and
deep dreams left behind.

They stood, Marie and Joseph, in the warm silent yard,
among the stones, between the walls. Far over in one
corner a little man with high cheekbones, the milk colour
of the Spanish infiltration, thick glasses, a black coat, a
grey hat and grey, unpressed pants and neatly laced shoes,
moved about among the stones, supervising something or
other that another man in overalls was doing to a grave
with a shovel. The little man with glasses carried a thrice
folded newspaper under his left arm and had his hands in
his pockets.

'*Buenos días señora y señor!*' he said, when he finally
noticed Joseph and Marie and came to see them.

'Is this the place of *las momias*?' asked Joseph. 'They
do exist, do they not?'

'*Sí*, the mummies,' said the man. 'They exist and are
here. In the catacombs.'

'*Por favor*,' said Joseph. '*Yo quiero ver las momias,
sí*?'

'*Sí, señor.*'

'*Mi español es mucho estúpido, es muy malo*,' apologized Joseph.

'No, no, *señor*. You speak well! This way, please.'

He led between the flowered stones to a tomb near the wall shadows. It was a large flat tomb, flush with the gravel, with a thin kindling door flat on it, padlocked. It was unlocked and the wood door flung back rattling to one side. Revealed was a round hole the circled interior of which contained steps which screwed into the earth.

Before Joseph could move, his wife had set her foot on the first step. 'Here,' he said. 'Me first.'

'No. That's all right,' she said, and went down and around in a darkening spiral until the earth vanished her. She moved carefully, for the steps were hardly enough to contain a child's feet. It got dark and she heard the caretaker stepping after her, at her ears, and then it got light again. They stepped out into a long whitewashed hall twenty feet under the earth, dimly lit by a few small gothic windows high in the arched ceiling. The hall was fifty yards long, ending on the left in a double door in which were set tall crystal panes and a sign forbidding entrance. On the right end of the hall was a large stack of white rods and round white stones.

'The soldiers who fought for Father Morelos,' said the caretaker.

They walked to the vast pile. They were neatly put in place, bone on bone, like firewood, and on top was a mound of a thousand dry skulls.

'I don't mind skulls and bones,' said Marie. 'There's nothing even vaguely human to them. I'm not scared of skulls and bones. They're like something insectile. If a child was raised and didn't know he had a skeleton in him, he wouldn't think anything of bones, would he? That's how it is with me. Everything human has been scraped off *these*. There's nothing familiar left to be horrible. In order for a thing to be horrible it has to suffer a change you can recognize. This isn't changed. They're still skeletons, like they always were. The part that changed is gone, and so there's nothing to show for it. Isn't that interesting?'

Joseph nodded.

She was quite brave now.

'Well,' she said, 'let's see the mummies.'

'Here, *señora*,' said the caretaker.

He took them far down the hall away from the stack of bones and when Joseph paid him a peso he unlocked the forbidden crystal doors and opened them wide and they looked into an even longer, dimly lighted hall in which stood the people.

They waited inside the door in a long line under the arch-roofed ceiling, fifty-five of them against one wall, on the left, fifty-five of them against the right wall, and five of them way down at the very end.

'Mister Interlocutor!' said Joseph, briskly.

They resembled nothing more than those preliminary erections of a sculptor, the wire frame, the first tendons of clay, the muscles, and a thin lacquer of skin. They were unfinished, all one hundred and fifteen of them.

They were parchment-coloured and the skin was stretched as if to dry, from bone to bone. The bodies were intact, only the watery humours had evaporated from them.

'The climate,' said the caretaker. 'It preserves them. Very dry.'

'How long have they been here?' asked Joseph.

'Some one year, some five, *señor*, some ten, some seventy.'

There was an embarrassment of horror. You started with the first man on your right, hooked and wired upright against the wall, and he was not good to look upon, and you went on to the woman next to him who was unbelievable and then to a man who was horrendous and then to a woman who was very sorry she was dead and in such a place as this.

'What are they doing here?' said Joseph.

'Their relatives did not pay the rent upon their graves.'

'Is there a rent?'

'*Sí, señor*. Twenty pesos a year. Or, if they desire the permanent interment, one hundred seventy pesos. But our people, they are very poor, as you must know, and one hundred seventy pesos is as much as many of them make in two years. So they carry their dead here and place them into the earth for one year, and the twenty pesos are paid, with fine intentions of paying each year and each year, but each year and each year after the first year they have a *burro* to buy or a new mouth to feed, or maybe three new mouths, and the dead, after all, are not hungry, and the dead, after all, can pull no ploughs; or there is a new wife or there is a roof in need of mending, and the dead, remember, can be in no beds with a man, and the dead, you understand, can keep no rain off one, and so it is that the dead are not paid up upon their rent.'

'*Then* what happens? Are you listening, Marie?' said Joseph.

Marie counted the bodies. One, two, three, four, five, six, seven, eight. 'What?' she said, quietly.

'Are you listening?'

'I think so. What? Oh, yes! I'm listening.'

Eight, nine, ten, eleven, twelve, thirteen.

'Well, then,' said the little man, 'I call a *trabajando* and with his delicate shovel at the end of the first year he does dig and dig and dig down. How deep do you think we dig, *señor*?'

'Six feet. That's the usual depth.'

'Ah, no, ah, no. There, *señor*, you would be wrong. Knowing that after the first year the rent is liable not to be paid, we bury the poorest two feet down. It is less work, you understand? Of course, we must judge by the family who own a body. Some of them we bury sometimes three, sometimes four feet deep, sometimes five, sometimes six, depending on how rich the family is, depending on what the chances are we won't have to dig him from out his place a year later. And, let me tell you, *señor*, when we bury a man the whole six feet deep we are very certain of his staying. We have never dug up a six-foot-buried one yet, that is the accuracy with which we know the money of the people.'

Twenty-one, twenty-two, twenty-three. Marie's lips moved with a small whisper.

'And the bodies which are dug up are placed down here against the wall, with the other *compañeros*.'

'Do the relatives know the bodies are here?'

'*Sí*.' The small man pointed. 'This one, *yo veo*? It is new. It has been here but one year. His *madre y padre* know him to be here. But have they money? Ah, no.'

'Isn't that rather gruesome for his parents?'

The little man was earnest. 'They never think of it,' he said.

'Did you hear that, Marie?'

'What?' Thirty, thirty-one, thirty-two, thirty-three, thirty-four. 'Yes. They never think of it.'

'What if the rent is paid again, after a lapse?' inquired Joseph.

'In that time,' said the caretaker, 'the bodies are reburied for as many years as are paid.'

'Sounds like blackmail,' said Joseph.

The little man shrugged, hands in pockets. 'We must live.'

'You are certain no one can pay the one hundred seventy pesos all at once,' said Joseph. 'So in this way you get them for twenty pesos a year, year after year, for maybe thirty years. If they don't pay, you threaten to stand *mamacita* or little *niño* in the catacomb.'

'We must live,' said the little man.

Fifty-one, fifty-two, fifty-three.

Marie counted in the centre of the long corridor, the standing dead on all sides of her.

They were screaming.

They looked as if they had leaped, snapped upright in their graves, clutched hands over their shrivelled bosoms and screamed, jaws wide, tongues out, nostrils flared.

And been frozen that way.

All of them had open mouths. Theirs was a perpetual screaming. They were dead and they knew it. In every raw fibre and evaporated organ they knew it.

She stood listening to them scream.

They say dogs hear sounds humans never hear, sounds so many decibels higher than normal hearing that they seem non-existent.

The corridor swarmed with screams. Screams poured from terror-yawned lips and dry tongues, screams you couldn't hear because they were so high.

Joseph walked up to one standing body.

'Say "ah",' he said.

Sixty-five, sixty-six, sixty-seven, counted Marie, among the screams.

'Here is an interesting one,' said the proprietor.

They saw a woman with arms flung to her head, mouth wide, teeth intact, whose hair was wildly flourished, long and shimmery on her head. Her eyes were small pale white-blue eggs in her skull.

'Sometimes, this happens. This woman, she is a cataleptic. One day she falls down upon the earth, but is really not dead, for, deep in her, the little drum of her heart beats and beats, so dim one cannot hear. So she was buried in the graveyard in a fine inexpensive box . . .'

'Didn't you know she was cataleptic?'

'Her sisters knew. But this time they thought her at last dead. And funerals are hasty things in this warm town.'

'She was buried a few hours after her "death"?'

'*Sí*, the same. All of this, as you see her here, we would

never have known, if a year later her sisters, having other things to buy, had not refused the rent on her burial. So we dug very quietly down and loosed the box and took it up and opened the top of her box and laid it aside and looked in upon her –'

Marie stared.

This woman had wakened under the earth. She had torn, shrieked, clubbed at the box-lid with fists, died of suffocation, in this attitude, hands flung over her gaping face, horror-eyed, hair wild.

'Be pleased, *señor*, to find that difference between *her* hands and these other ones,' said the caretaker. 'Their peaceful fingers at their hips, quiet as little roses. Hers? Ah, hers! are jumped up, very wildly, as if to pound the lid free!'

'Couldn't rigor mortis do that?'

'Believe me, *señor*, rigor mortis pounds upon no lids. Rigor mortis screams not like this, nor twists nor wrestles to rip free nails, *señor*, or prise boards loose hunting for air, *señor*. All these others are open of mouth, *sí*, because they were not injected with the fluids of embalming, but theirs is a simple screaming of muscles, *señor*. This *señorita*, here, hers is the *muerte horrible.*'

Marie walked, scuffling her shoes, turning first this way, then that. Naked bodies. Long ago the clothes had whispered away. The fat women's breasts were lumps of yeasty dough left in the dust. The men's loins were indrawn, withered orchids.

'Mr Grimace and Mr Gape,' said Joseph.

He pointed his camera at two men who seemed in conversation, mouths in mid-sentence, hands gesticulant and stiffened over some long-dissolved gossip.

Joseph clicked the shutter, rolled the film, focused the camera on another body, clicked the shutter, rolled the film, walked on to another.

Eighty-one, eighty-two, eighty-three. Jaws down, tongues

out like jeering children, eyes pale brown-irised in up-
clenched sockets. Hairs, waxed and prickled by sunlight,
each sharp as quills embedded on the lips, the cheeks,
the eyelids, the brows. Little beards on chins and bosoms
and loins. Flesh like drumheads and manuscripts and crisp
bread dough. The women, huge ill-shaped tallow things,
death-melted. The insane hair of them, like nests made
and unmade and remade. Teeth, each single, each fine,
each perfect, in jaw. Eighty-six, eighty-seven, eighty-
eight. A rushing of Marie's eyes. Down the corridor,
flicking. Counting, rushing, never stopping. On! Quick!
Ninety-one, ninety-two, ninety-three! Here was a man,
his stomach open, like a tree hollow where you dropped
your child love-letters when you were eleven! Her eyes
entered the hole in the space under his ribs. She peeked
in. He looked like an Erector set inside. The spine, the
pelvic plates. The rest was tendon, parchment, bone,
eye, beardy jaw, ear, stupefied nostril. And this ragged
eaten cincture in his navel into which a pudding might
be spooned. Ninety-seven, ninety-eight! Names, places,
dates, things!

'This woman died in childbirth!'

Like a little hungry doll, the prematurely born child was
wired, dangling, to her wrist.

'This was a soldier. His uniform still half on him –'

Marie's eyes slammed the furthest wall after a back-
forth, back-forth swinging from horror to horror, from
skull to skull, beating from rib to rib, staring with hypnotic
fascination at paralysed, loveless, fleshless loins, at men
made into women by evaporation, at women made into
dugged swine. The fearful ricochet of vision, growing,
growing, taking impetus from swollen breast to raving
mouth, wall to wall, wall to wall, again, again, like a
ball hurled in a game, caught in the incredible teeth,
spat in a scream across the corridor to be caught in
claws, lodged between thin teats, the whole standing

chorus invisibly chanting the game on, on, the wild game of sight recoiling, rebounding, reshuttling on down the inconceivable procession, through a montage of erected horrors that ended finally and for all time when vision crashed against the corridor ending with one last scream from all present!

Marie turned and shot her vision far down to where the spiral steps walked up into sunlight. How talented was death. How many expressions and manipulations of hand, face, body, no two alike. They stood like the naked pipes of a vast derelict calliope, their mouths cut into frantic vents. And now the great hand of mania descended upon all keys at once, and the long calliope screamed upon one hundred-throated, unending scream.

Click went the camera and Joseph rolled the film. Click went the camera and Joseph rolled the film.

Moreno, Morelos, Cantine, Gomez, Gutierrez, Villa-nousul, Ureta, Licon, Navarro, Iturbi; Jorge, Filomena, Nena, Manuel, José, Tomás, Ramóna. This man walked and this man sang and this man had three wives; and this man died of this, and that of that, and the third from another thing, and the fourth was shot, and the fifth was stabbed and the sixth fell straight down dead; and the seventh drank deep and died dead, and the eighth died in love, and the ninth fell from his horse, and the tenth coughed blood, and the eleventh stopped his heart, and the twelfth used to laugh much, and the thirteenth was a dancing one, and the fourteenth was most beautiful of all, the fifteenth had ten children and the sixteenth is one of those children as is the seventeenth; and the eighteenth was Tomás and did well with his guitar; the next three cut maize in their fields, had three lovers each; the twenty-second was never loved; the twenty-third sold *tortillas*, patting and shaping them each at the kerb before the Opera House with her little charcoal stove; and the twenty-fourth beat his wife and now she walks proudly in the town and is merry with new men and here he stands bewildered by this unfair thing, and the twenty-fifth drank several quarts of river with his lungs and was pulled forth in a net, and the twenty-sixth was a great thinker and his brain now sleeps like a burnt plum in his skull.

'I'd like a colour shot of each, and his or her name and how he or she died,' said Joseph. 'It would be an amazing, an ironical book to publish. The more you think, the more it grows on you. Their life histories and then a picture of each of them standing here.'

He tapped each chest, softly. They gave off hollow sounds, like someone rapping on a door.

Marie pushed her way through screams that hung net-wise across her path. She walked evenly, in the corridor centre, not slow, but not too fast, towards the spiral stair, not looking to either side. Click went the camera behind her.

'You have room down here for more?' said Joseph.

'*Sí, señor*. Many more.'

'Wouldn't want to be next in line, next on your waiting list.'

'Ah, no, *señor*, one would not wish to be next.'

'How are chances of buying one of these?'

'Oh, no, no, *señor*. Oh, no, no. Oh no, *señor*.'

'I'll pay you fifty pesos.'

'Oh, no, *señor*, no, no, *señor*.'

In the market, the remainder of candy skulls from the Death Fiesta were sold from flimsy little tables. Women hung with black *rebozos* sat quietly, now and then speaking one word to each other, the sweet sugar skeletons, the saccharine corpses and white candy skulls at their elbows. Each skull had a name on top in gold candy curlicue; José or Carmen or Ramón or Teña or Guiermo or Rosa. They sold cheap. The Death Festival was gone. Joseph paid a peso and got two candy skulls.

Marie stood in the narrow street. She saw the candy skulls and Joseph and the dark ladies who put the skulls in a bag.

'Not *really*,' said Marie.

'Why not?' said Joseph.

'Not after just *now*,' she said.

'In the catacombs?'

She nodded.

He said, 'But these are good.'

'They look poisonous.'

'Just because they're skull-shaped?'

'No. The sugar itself looks raw, how do you know what kind of people made them, they might have the colic.'

'My dear Marie, all people in Mexico have colic,' he said.

'You can eat them both,' she said.

'Alas, poor Yorick,' he said, peeking into the bag.

They walked along a street that was held between high buildings in which were yellow window frames and pink iron grilles and the smell of tamales came from them and the sound of lost fountains splashing on hidden tiles and little birds clustering and peeping in bamboo cages and someone playing Chopin on a piano.

'Chopin, here,' said Joseph. 'How strange and swell.' He looked up. 'I like that bridge. Hold this.' He handed her the candy bag while he clicked a picture of a red bridge spanning two white buildings with a man walking on it, a red serape on his shoulder. 'Fine,' said Joseph.

Marie walked looking at Joseph, looking away from him and then back at him, her lips moving but not speaking, her eyes fluttering, a little neck muscle under her chin like a wire, a little nerve in her brow ticking. She passed the candy bag from one hand to the other. She stepped up a kerb, leaned back somehow, gestured, said something to restore balance, and dropped the bag.

'For Christ's sake.' Joseph snatched up the bag. 'Look what you've done! Clumsy!'

'I should have broken my ankle,' she said, 'I suppose.'

'These were the best skulls; both of them smashed; I wanted to save them for friends up home.'

'I'm sorry,' she said, vaguely.

'For God's sake, oh, damn it to hell.' He scowled into the bag. 'I might not find any more good as these. Oh, I don't know, I give up!'

The wind blew and they were alone in the street, he staring down into the shattered debris in the bag, she with the street shadows all around her, sun on the other side of the street, nobody about, and the world far away, the two of them alone, two thousand miles from anywhere, on a street in a false town behind which was nothing and around which was nothing but blank desert and circled hawks. On top of the State Opera House, a block down, the golden Greek statues stood sunbright and high, and in a beer place a shouting phonograph cried AY, MARIMBA . . . *corazón* . . . and all kinds of alien words which the wind stirred away.

Joseph twisted the bag shut, stuck it furiously in his pocket.

They walked back to the two-thirty lunch at the hotel.

He sat at the table with Marie, sipping Albondigas soup from his moving spoon, silently. Twice she commented cheerfully upon the wall murals and he looked at her steadily and sipped. The bag of cracked skulls lay on the table . . .

'*Señora* . . .'

The soup plates were cleared by a brown hand. A large plate of *enchiladas* was set down.

Marie looked at the plate.

There were sixteen *enchiladas*.

She put her fork and knife out to take one and stopped. She put her fork and knife down at each side of her plate.

She glanced at the walls and then at her husband and then at the sixteen *enchiladas*.

Sixteen. One by one. A long row of them, crowded together.

She counted them.

One, two, three, four, five, six.

Joseph took one on his plate and ate it.

Six, seven, eight, nine, ten, eleven.

She put her hands on her lap.

Twelve, thirteen, fourteen, fifteen, sixteen. She finished counting.

'I'm not hungry,' she said.

He placed another *enchilada* before himself. It had an interior clothed in a papyrus of corn *tortilla*. It was slender and it was one of many he cut and placed in his mouth and she chewed it for him in her mind's mouth, and squeezed her eyes tight.

'Eh?' he asked.

'Nothing,' she said.

Thirteen *enchiladas* remained, like tiny bundles, like scrolls.

He ate five more.

'I don't feel well,' she said.

'Feel better if you ate,' he said.

'No.'

He finished, then opened the sack and took out one of the half-demolished skulls.

'Not *here*?' she said.

'Why not?' And he put one sugar socket to his lips, chewing. 'Not bad,' he said, thinking the taste. He popped in another section of the skull. 'Not bad at all.'

She looked at the name on the skull he was eating.

Marie, it said.

It was tremendous, the way she helped him pack. In those newsreels you see men leap off diving-boards into pools, only, a moment later when the reel is reversed, to jump back up in airy fantasy to alight once more safe on the diving-board. Now, as Joseph watched, the suits and dresses flew into their boxes and cases, the hats were like birds darting, clapped into round, bright hatboxes, the shoes seemed to run across the floor like mice to leap into valises. The suitcases banged shut, the hasps clicked, the keys turned.

'There!' she cried. 'All packed! Oh, Joe, I'm so glad you let me change your mind.'

She started for the door.

'Here, let me help,' he said.

'They're not heavy,' she said.

'But you never carry suitcases. You never have. I'll call a boy.'

'Nonsense,' she said, breathless with the weight of the valises.

A boy seized the cases outside the door. '*Señora, por favor!*'

'Have we forgotten anything?' He looked under the two beds, he went out on the balcony and gazed at the plaza, came in, went to the bathroom, looked in the cabinet and on the washbowl. 'Here,' he said, coming out and handing her something. 'You forgot your wrist watch.'

'Did I?' She put it on and went out the door.

'I don't know,' he said. 'It's damn late in the day to be moving out.'

'It's only three-thirty,' she said. 'Only three-thirty.'

'I don't know,' he said, doubtfully.

He looked around the room, stepped out, closed the door, locked it, went downstairs, jingling the keys.

She was outside in the car already, settled in, her coat folded on her lap, her gloved hands folded on the coat. He came out, supervised the loading of what luggage remained into the trunk receptacle, came to the front door and tapped on the window. She unlocked it and let him in.

'Well, here we *go*!' she cried with a laugh, her face rosy, her eyes frantically bright. She was leaning forward as if by this movement she might set the car rolling merrily down the hill. 'Thank you, darling, for letting me get the refund on the money you paid for our room tonight. I'm sure we'll like it much better in Guadalajara tonight. Thank you!'

'Yeah,' he said.

Inserting the ignition keys he stepped on the starter.

Nothing happened.

He stepped on the starter again. Her mouth twitched.

'It needs warming,' she said. 'It was a cold night last night.'

He tried it again. Nothing.

Marie's hands tumbled on her lap.

He tried it six more times. 'Well,' he said, lying back, ceasing.

'Try it again, next time it'll work,' she said.

'It's no use,' he said. 'Something's wrong.'

'Well, you've got to try it once more.'

He tried it once more.

'It'll work, I'm sure,' she said. 'Is the ignition on?'

'Is the ignition on,' he said. 'Yes, it's *on*.'

'It doesn't look like it's on,' she said.

'It's on.' He showed her by twisting the key.

'*Now* try it,' she said.

'There,' he said, when nothing happened. 'I *told* you.'

'You're not doing it right; it almost caught that time,' she cried.

'I'll wear out the battery, and God knows where you can buy a battery here.'

'Wear it out, then. I'm sure it'll start next time!'

'Well, if you're so good, you try it.' He slipped from the car and beckoned her over behind the wheel. 'Go ahead!'

She bit her lips and settled behind the wheel. She did things with her hands that were like a little mystic ceremony; with moves of hands and body she was trying to overcome gravity, friction and every other natural law. She patted the starter with her toeless shoe. The car remained solemnly quiet. A little squeak came out of Marie's tightened lips. She rammed the starter home and there was a clear smell in the air as she fluttered the choke.

'You've flooded it,' he said. 'Fine! Get back over on your side, will you?'

He got three boys to push and they started the car downhill. He jumped in to steer. The car rolled swiftly, bumping and rattling. Marie's face glowed expectantly. 'This'll start it!' she said.

Nothing started. They rolled quietly into the filling station at the bottom of the hill, bumping softly on the cobbles, and stopped by the tanks.

She sat there, saying nothing, and when the attendant came from the station her door was locked, the window up, and he had to come around on the husband's side to make his query.

The mechanic arose from the car engine, scowled at Joseph and they spoke together in Spanish, quietly.

She rolled the window down and listened.

'What's he say?' she demanded.

The two men talked on.

'What does he say?' she asked.

The dark mechanic waved at the engine. Joseph nodded and they conversed.

'What's wrong?' Marie wanted to know.

Joseph frowned over at her. 'Wait a moment, will you? I can't listen to both of you.'

The mechanic took Joseph's elbow. They said many words.

'What's he saying now?' she asked.

'He says —' said Joseph, and was lost as the Mexican

took him over to the engine and bent him down in earnest discovery.

'How much will it cost?' she cried, out the window, around at their bent backs.

The mechanic spoke to Joseph.

'Fifty pesos,' said Joseph.

'How long will it take?' cried his wife.

Joseph asked the mechanic. The man shrugged and they argued for five minutes.

'How long will it take?' said Marie.

The discussion continued.

The sun went down the sky. She looked at the sun upon the trees that stood high by the cemetery yard. The shadows rose and rose until the valley was enclosed and only the sky was clear and untouched and blue.

'Two days, maybe three,' said Joseph, turning to Marie.

'Two days! Can't he fix it so we can just go on to the next town and have the rest done there?'

Joseph asked the man. The man replied.

Joseph said to his wife, 'No, he'll have to do the entire job.'

'Why, that's silly, it's so silly, he doesn't either, he doesn't really have to do it all, you tell him that, Joe, tell him that, he can hurry and fix it –'

The two men ignored her. They were talking earnestly again.

This time it was all in very slow motion. The unpacking of the suitcases. He did his own, she left hers by the door.

'I don't need anything,' she said, leaving it locked.

'You'll need your nightgown,' he said.

'I'll sleep naked,' she said.

'Well, it isn't my fault,' he said. 'That damned car.'

'You can go down and watch them work on it, later,' she said. She sat on the edge of the bed. They were in a new room. She had refused to return to their old room.

She said she couldn't stand it. She wanted a new room so it would seem they were in a new hotel in a new city. So this was a new room, with a view of the alley and the sewer system instead of the plaza and the drum-box trees. 'You go down and supervise the work, Joe. If you don't you know they'll take weeks!' She looked at him. 'You should be down there now, instead of standing around.'

'I'll go down,' he said.

'I'll go down with you. I want to buy some magazines.'

'You won't find any American magazines in a town like this.'

'I can look, can't I?'

'Besides, we haven't much money,' he said. 'I don't want to have to wire my bank. It takes a god-awful time and it's not worth the bother.'

'I can at least have my magazines,' she said.

'Maybe one or two,' he said.

'As many as I want,' she said, feverishly, on the bed.

'For God's sake, you've got a million magazines in the car now, *Posts, Collier's, Mercury, Atlantic Monthlys, Barnaby, Superman*! You haven't read half of the articles.'

'But they're not new,' she said. 'They're not new. I've *looked* at them and after you've looked at a thing, I don't know –'

'Try reading them instead of looking at them,' he said.

As they came downstairs night was in the plaza.

'Give me a few pesos,' she said, and he gave her some. 'Teach me to say about magazines in Spanish,' she said.

'*Quiero una publicación americana*,' he said, walking swiftly.

She repeated it, stumblingly, and laughed. 'Thanks.'

He went on ahead to the mechanic's shop, and she turned in at the nearest *farmacia botica*, and all the magazines racked before her there were alien colours and alien names. She read the titles with swift moves of her eyes and looked at the old man behind the counter.

'Do you have American magazines?' she asked in English, embarrassed to use the Spanish words.

The old man stared at her.

'*Habla inglés?*' she asked.

'No, *señorita.*'

She tried to think of the right words. '*Quiero* – no!' She stopped. She started again. '*Americano* – uh – *magg-ah-zeen-as?*'

'Oh, no, *señorita*!'

Her hands opened wide at her waist, then closed, like mouths. Her mouth opened and closed. The shop had a veil over it, in her eyes. Here she was and here were the small baked adobe people to whom she could say nothing and from whom she could get no words she understood, and she was in a town of people who said no words to her and she said no words to them except in blushing confusion and bewilderment. And the town was circled by desert and time, and home was far away, far away in another life.

She whirled and fled.

Shop following shop she found no magazines save those giving bullfights in blood on their covers or murdered people or lace-confection priests. But at last three poor copies of the *Post* were bought with much display and loud laughter and she gave the vendor of this small shop a handsome tip.

Rushing out with the *Posts* eagerly on her bosom in both hands she hurried along the narrow walk, took a skip over the gutter, ran across the street, sang la-la, jumped on to the further walk, made another little scamper with her feet, smiled an inside smile, moving along swiftly, pressing the magazines tightly to her, half-closing her eyes, breathing the charcoal evening air, feeling the wind watering past her ears.

Starlight tinkled in golden nuclei off the highly perched Greek figures atop the State theatre. A man shambled by in the shadow, balancing upon his head a basket. The basket contained bread loaves.

She saw the man and the balanced basket and suddenly she did not move and there was no inside smile, nor did her hands clasp tight the magazines. She watched the man walk, with one hand of his gently poised up to tap the basket any time it unbalanced, and down the street he dwindled, while the magazines slipped from Marie's fingers and scattered on the walk.

Snatching them up, she ran into the hotel and almost fell going upstairs.

She sat in the room. The magazines were piled on each side of her and in a circle at her feet. She had made a little castle with portcullises of words and into this she was withdrawn. All about her were the magazines she had bought and bought and looked at and looked at on other days, and these were the outer barrier, and upon the inside of the barrier, upon her lap, as yet unopened, but her hands were trembling to open them and read and read and read again with hungry eyes, were the three battered *Post* magazines. She opened the first page. She would go through them page by page, line by line, she decided. Not a line would go unnoticed, a comma unread, every little ad and every colour would be fixed by her. And – she smiled with discovery – in those other magazines at her feet were still advertisements and cartoons she had neglected – there would be little morsels of stuff for her to reclaim and utilize later.

She would read this first *Post* tonight, yes tonight she would read this first delicious *Post*. Page on page she would eat it and tomorrow night, if there was going to be a tomorrow night, but maybe there wouldn't be a tomorrow night here, maybe the motor would start and there'd be odours of exhaust and the round hum of rubber tyre on road and wind riding in the window and pennanting her hair – but, suppose, just suppose there would BE a tomorrow night here, in this room. Well, then, there would be two more *Posts*, one for tomorrow night, and the next for the next night. How neatly she said it to herself with her mind's tongue. She turned the first page.

She turned the second page. Her eyes moved over it and over it and her fingers unknown to her slipped under the next page and flickered it in preparation for turning, and the watch ticked on her wrist, and time passed and she sat turning pages, turning pages, hungrily seeing the framed people in the pictures, people who lived in another land in another world where neons bravely held off the night with crimson bars and the smells were home smells and the people talked good fine words and here she was turning the pages, and all the lines went across and down and the pages flew under her hands, making a fan. She threw down the first *Post*, seized on and riffled through the second in half an hour, threw that down, took up the third, threw that down a good fifteen minutes later and found herself breathing, breathing stiffly in her body and out of her mouth. She put her hand up to the back of her neck.

Somewhere, a soft breeze was blowing.

The hairs along the back of her neck slowly stood upright.

She touched them with one pale hand as one touches the nape of a dandelion.

Outside, in the plaza, the street lights rocked like crazy flashlights on a wind. Papers ran through the gutters in sheep flocks. Shadows pencilled and slashed under the bucketing lamps now this way, now that, here a shadow one instant, there a shadow next, now no shadows, all cold light, now no light, all cold blue-black shadow. The lamps creaked on their high metal hasps.

In the room her hands began to tremble. She saw them tremble. Her body began to tremble. Under the bright bright print of the brightest, loudest skirt she could find to put on especially for tonight, in which she had whirled and cavorted feverishly before the coffin-sized mirror, beneath the rayon skirt the body was all wire and tendon and excitation. Her teeth chattered and fused and chattered. Her lipstick smeared, one lip crushing another.

Joseph knocked on the door.

They got ready for bed. He had returned with the news that something had been done to the car and it would take time, he'd go watch them tomorrow.

'But don't knock on the door,' she said, standing before the mirror as she undressed.

'Leave it unlocked then,' he said.

'I want it locked. But don't rap. Call.'

'What's wrong with rapping?' he said.

'It sounds funny,' she said.

'What do you mean, funny?'

She wouldn't say. She was looking at herself in the mirror and she was naked, with her hands at her sides, and there were her breasts and her hips and her entire body, and it moved, it felt the floor under it and the walls and air around it, and the breasts could know hands if hands were put there, and the stomach would make no hollow echo if touched.

'For God's sake,' he said, 'don't stand there admiring yourself.' He was in bed. 'What are you doing?' he said. 'What're you putting your hands up that way for, over your face?'

He put the lights out.

She could not speak to him for she knew no words that he knew and he said nothing to her that she understood, and she walked to her bed and slipped into it and he lay with his back to her in his bed and he was like one of these brown-baked people of this far-away town upon the moon, and the real earth was off somewhere where it would take a star-flight to reach it. If only he could speak with her and she to him tonight, how good the night might be, and how easy to breathe and how lax the vessels of blood in her ankles and in her wrists and the under-arms, but there was no speaking and the night was ten thousand tickings and ten thousand twistings of the blankets, and the pillow was like a tiny white warm stove under-cheek, and the blackness of the room was a mosquito netting draped all about so that a turn entangled her in it. If only there was one word, one word between them. But there was no word and the veins did not rest easy in the wrists and the heart was a bellows for ever blowing upon a little coal of fear, for ever illumining and making it into a cherry light, again, pulse, and again, an ingrown light which her inner eyes stared upon with unwanting fascination. The lungs did not rest but were exercised as if she were a drowned person and she herself performing artificial respiration to keep the last life going. And all of these things were lubricated by the sweat of her glowing body, and she was glued fast between the heavy blankets like something pressed, smashed, redolently moist between the white pages of a heavy book.

And as she lay this way the long hours of midnight came when again she was a child. She lay, now and again thumping her heart in tambourine hysteria, then, quieting, the slow sad thought of bronze childhood when everything was sun on green trees and sun on water and sun on blond child hair. Faces flowed by on merry-go-rounds of memory, a face rushing to meet her, facing her, and away to the right; another, whirling in from the left, a quick fragment of lost conversation, and out to the right. Around and round. Oh, the night was very long. She consoled herself by thinking of the car starting tomorrow, the throttling sound and the power sound and the road moving under, and she smiled in the dark with pleasure. But then, suppose the car did *not* start? She crumpled in the dark, like a burning, withering paper. All the folds and corners of her clenched in about her and tick tick tick went the wrist watch, tick tick tick and another tick to wither on . . .

Morning. She looked at her husband lying straight and easy on his bed. She let her hand laze down at the cool space between the beds. All night her hand had hung in that cold empty interval between. Once she had put her hand out towards him, stretching, but the space was just a little too long, she couldn't reach him. She had snapped her hand back, hoping he hadn't heard the movement of her silent reaching.

There he lay now. His eyes gently closed, the lashes softly interlocked like clasped fingers. Breathing so quietly you could scarce see his ribs move. As usual, by this time of morning, he had worked out of his pyjamas. His naked chest was revealed from the waist up. The rest of him lay under cover. His head lay on the pillow, in thoughtful profile.

There was a beard stubble on his chin.

The morning light showed the white of her eyes. They were the only things in the room in motion, in slow starts and stops, tracing the anatomy of the man across from her.

Each little hair was perfect on the chin and cheeks. A tiny hole of sunlight from the window-shade lay on his chin and picked out, like the spikes of a music-box cylinder, each little hair on his face.

His wrists on either side of him had little curly black hairs, each perfect, each separate and shiny and glittering.

The hair on his head was intact, strand by dark strand, down to the roots. The ears were beautifully carved. The teeth were intact behind the lips.

'Joseph!' she screamed.

'Joseph!' she screamed again, flailing up in terror.

Bong! Bong! Bong! went the bell thunder across the street, from the great tiled cathedral!

Pigeons rose in a papery white whirl, like so many

magazines fluttered past the window! The pigeons circled the plaza, spiralling up. Bong! went the bells! Honk went a taxi horn! Far away down an alley a music box played *Cielito Lindo*.

All these faded into the dripping of the faucet in the bath sink.

Joseph opened his eyes.

His wife sat on her bed, staring at him.

'I thought –' he said. He blinked. 'No.' He shut his eyes and shook his head. 'Just the bells.' A sigh. 'What time is it?'

'I don't know. Yes, I do. Eight o'clock.'

'Good God,' he murmured, turning over. 'We can sleep three more hours.'

'You've got to get up!' she cried.

'Nobody's up. They won't be to work at the garage until ten, you know that, you can't rush these people; keep quiet now.'

'But you've got to get up,' she said.

He half-turned. Sunlight prickled black hairs into bronze on his upper lip. '*Why?* Why, in Christ's name, do I *have* to get up?'

'You need a shave!' she almost screamed.

He moaned. 'So I have to get up and lather myself at eight in the morning because I need a shave.'

'Well, you do need one.'

'I'm not shaving again till we reach Texas.'

'You can't go around looking like a tramp!'

'I can and will. I've shaved every morning for thirty goddamn mornings and put on a tie and had a crease in my pants. From now on, no pants, no ties, no shaving, no nothing.'

He yanked the covers over his ears so violently that he pulled the blankets off one of his naked legs.

The leg hung upon the rim of the bed, warm white in the sunlight, each little black hair – perfect.

Her eyes widened, focused, stared upon it.
She put her hand over her mouth, tight.

He went in and out of the hotel all day. He did not shave.
He walked along the plaza tiles below. He walked so slowly
she wanted to throw a lightning bolt out of the window and
hit him. He paused and talked to the hotel manager below,
under a drum-cut tree, shifting his shoes on the pale blue
plaza tiles. He looked at birds on trees and saw how the
State Theatre statues were dressed in fresh morning gilt,
and stood on the corner, watching the traffic carefully.
There was no traffic! He was standing there on purpose,
taking his time, not looking back at her. Why didn't he run,
lope down the alley, down the hill to the garage, pound
on the doors, threaten the mechanics, lift them by their
pants, shove them into the car motor! He stood instead,
watching the ridiculous traffic pass. A hobbled swine, a
man on a bike, a 1927 Ford, and three half-nude children.
Go, go, go, she screamed silently, and almost smashed the
window.

He sauntered across the street. He went around the
corner. All the way down to the garage he'd stop at
windows, read signs, look at pictures, handle pottery.
Maybe he'd stop in for a beer. God, yes, a beer.

She walked in the plaza, took the sun, hunted for more
magazines. She cleaned her fingernails, burnished them,
took a bath, walked again in the plaza, ate very little, and
returned to the room to feed upon her magazines.

She did not lie down. She was afraid to. Each time
she did she fell into a half-dream, half-drowse in which
all her childhood was revealed in a helpless melancholy.
Old friends, children she hadn't seen or thought of in
twenty years filled her mind. And she thought of things
she wanted to do and had never done. She had meant to
call Lila Holdridge for the past eight years since college,
but somehow she never had. What friends they had been!

Dear Lila! She thought, when lying down, of all the books, the fine new and old books, she had meant to buy and might never buy now and read. How she loved books and the smell of books. She thought of a thousand old sad things. She'd wanted to own the Oz books all her life, yet had never bought them. Why *not*? while yet there was life! The first thing she'd do would be to buy them when she got back to New York! And she'd call Lila immediately! And she'd see Bert and Jimmy and Helen and Louise, and go back to Illinois and walk around in her childhood place and see the things to be seen there. If she got back to the States. If. Her heart beat painfully in her, paused, held on to itself, and beat again. *If* she ever got back.

She lay listening to her heart, critically.

Thud and a thud and a thud. Pause. Thud and a thud and a thud. Pause.

What if it should stop while she was listening?

Silence inside her.

'Joseph!'

She leaped up. She grabbed at her breasts as if to squeeze, to pump, to start the silent heart again!

It opened in her, closed, rattled and beat nervously, twenty rapid, shot-like times!

She sank on to the bed. What if it should stop again and not start? What would she think? What would there be to do? She'd die of fright, that's what. A joke; it was very humorous. Die of fright if you heard your heart stop. She would have to listen to it, keep it beating. She wanted to go home and see Lila and buy the books and dance again and walk in Central Park and – listen –

Thud and a thud and a thud. Pause.

Joseph knocked on the door. Joseph knocked on the door and the car was not repaired and there would be another night, and Joseph did not shave and each little hair was perfect on his chin, and the magazine shops were closed and there were no more magazines, and they ate supper, a little bit anyway for her, and he went out in the evening to walk in the town.

She sat once more in the chair and slow erections of hair rose as if a magnet were passed over her neck. She was very weak and could not move from the chair, and she had no body, she was only a heart-beat, a huge pulsation of warmth and ache between four walls of the room. Her eyes were hot and pregnant, swollen with child of terror behind the bellied, tautened lids.

Deeply inside herself, she felt the first little cog slip. Another night, another night, another night, she thought. And this will be longer than the last. The first little cog slipped, the pendulum missed a stroke. Followed by the second and third interrelated cogs. The cogs interlocked, a small with a little larger one, the little larger one with a bit larger one, the bit larger one with a large one, the large one with a huge one, the huge one with an immense one, the immense one with a titanic one . . .

A red ganglion, no bigger than a scarlet thread, snapped and quivered; a nerve, no greater than a red linen fibre, twisted. Deep in her one little mech was gone and the entire machine, imbalanced, was about to steadily shake itself to bits.

She didn't fight it. She let it quake and terrorize her and knock the sweat off her brow and jolt down her spine and flood her mouth with horrible wine. She felt as if a broken gyro tilted now this way, now that and blundered and trembled and whined in her. The colour fell from her face like light leaving a clicked-off bulb, the crystal cheeks of the bulb vessel showing veins and filaments all colourless . . .

Joseph was in the room, he had come in, but she didn't even hear him. He was in the room but it made no difference, he changed nothing with his coming. He was getting ready for bed and said nothing as he moved about and she said nothing but fell into the bed while he moved around in a smoke-filled space beyond her and once he spoke but she didn't hear him.

She timed it. Every five minutes she looked at her watch and the watch shook and time shook and the five fingers were fifteen moving, reassembling into five. The shaking never stopped. She called for water. She turned and turned upon the bed. The wind blew outside, cocking the lights and spilling bursts of illumination that hit buildings glancing sidelong blows, causing windows to glitter like opened eyes and shut swiftly as the light tilted in yet another direction. Downstairs, all was quiet after the dinner, no sounds came up into their silent room. He handed her a water glass.

'I'm cold, Joseph,' she said, lying deep in folds of cover.

'You're all right,' he said.

'No, I'm not. I'm not well. I'm afraid.'

'There's nothing to be afraid of.'

'I want to get on the train for the United States.'

'There's a train in León, but none here,' he said, lighting a new cigarette.

'Let's drive there.'

'In these taxis, with these drivers, and leave our car here?'

'Yes. I want to go.'

'You'll be all right in the morning.'

'I know I won't be. I'm not well.'

He said, 'It would cost hundreds of dollars to have the car shipped home.'

'I don't care. I have two hundred dollars in the bank at home. I'll pay for it. But, please, let's go home.'

'When the sun shines tomorrow you'll feel better, it's just that the sun's gone now.'

'Yes, the sun's gone and the wind's blowing,' she whispered, closing her eyes, turning her head, listening. 'Oh, what a lonely wind. Mexico's a strange land. All the jungles and deserts and lonely stretches, and here and there a little town, like this, with a few lights burning you could put out with a snap of your fingers . . .'

'It's a pretty big country,' he said.

'Don't these people ever get lonely?'

'They're used to it this way.'

'Don't they get afraid, then?'

'They have a religion for that.'

'I wish *I* had a religion.'

'The minute you get a religion you stop thinking,' he said. 'Believe in one thing too much and you have no room for new ideas.'

'Tonight,' she said, faintly, 'I'd like nothing more than to have no more room for new ideas, to stop thinking, to believe in one thing so much it leaves me no time to be afraid.'

'You're not afraid,' he said.

'If I had a religion,' she said, ignoring him, 'I'd have a lever with which to lift myself. But I haven't a lever now and I don't know how to lift myself.'

'Oh, for God's –' he mumbled to himself, sitting down.

'I used to have a religion,' she said.

'Baptist.'

'No, that was when I was twelve. I got over that. I mean – *later*.'

'You never told me.'

'You should have known,' she said.

'What religion? Plaster saints in the sacristy? Any special saint you liked to tell your beads to?'

'Yes.'

'And did he answer your prayers?'

'For a little while. Lately, no, never. Never any more. Not for years now. But I keep praying.'

'Which saint is this?'

'Saint Joseph.'

'Saint Joseph.' He got up and poured himself a glass of

water from the glass pitcher, and it was a lonely trickling sound in the room. 'My name.'

'Coincidence,' she said.

They looked at one another for a few moments.

He looked away. 'Plaster saints,' he said, drinking the water down.

After a while she said, 'Joseph?' He said, 'Yes?' and she said, 'Come hold my hand, will you?' 'Women,' he sighed. He came and held her hand. After a minute she drew her hand away, hid it under the blanket, leaving his hand empty behind. With her eyes closed she trembled the words, 'Never mind. It's not as nice as I can imagine it. It's really nice the way I can make you hold my hand in my mind.' 'Gods,' he said, and went into the bathroom. She turned off the light. Only the small crack of light under the bathroom door showed. She listened to her heart. It beat one hundred and fifty times a minute, steadily, and the little whining tremor was still in her marrow, as if each bone of her body had a blue-bottle fly imprisoned in it, hovering, buzzing, shaking, quivering deep, deep, deep. Her eyes reversed into herself, to watch the secret heart of herself pounding itself to pieces against the side of her chest.

Water ran in the bathroom. She heard him washing his teeth.

'Joseph!'

'Yes?' he said, behind the shut door.

'Come here.'

'What do you want?'

'I want you to promise me something, please, oh, please.'

'What is it?'

'Open the door, first.'

'What *is* it?' he demanded, behind the closed door.

'Promise me,' she said, and stopped.

'Promise you what?' he asked, after a long pause.

'Promise me,' she said, and couldn't go on. She lay

there. He said nothing. She heard the watch and her heart pounding together. A lantern creaked on the hotel exterior. 'Promise me, if anything – happens,' she heard herself say, muffled and paralysed, as if she were on one of the surrounding hills talking at him from the distance, '– if anything happens to me, you won't let me be buried here in the graveyard over those terrible catacombs!'

'Don't be foolish,' he said, behind the door.

'Promise me?' she said, eyes wide in the dark.

'Of all the foolish things to talk about.'

'Promise, *please* promise?'

'You'll be all right in the morning,' he said.

'Promise so I can sleep. I can sleep if only you'd say you wouldn't let me be put there. I don't want to be put there.'

'Honestly,' he said, out of patience.

'Please,' she said.

'Why should I promise anything so ridiculous?' he said. 'You'll be fine tomorrow. And besides, if you died, you'd look very pretty in the catacomb standing between Mr Grimace and Mr Gape, with a sprig of morning-glory in your hair.' And he laughed sincerely.

Silence. She lay there in the dark.

'Don't you think you'll look pretty there?' he asked, laughingly, behind the door.

She said nothing in the dark room.

'*Don't* you?' he said.

Somebody walked down below in the plaza, faintly, fading away.

'Eh?' he asked her, brushing his teeth.

She lay there, staring up at the ceiling, her breast rising and falling faster, faster, faster, the air going in and out, in and out her nostrils, a little trickle of blood coming from her clenched lips. Her eyes were very wide, her hands blindly constricted the bedclothes.

'Eh?' he said again behind the door.

She said nothing.

'Sure,' he talked to himself. 'Pretty as hell,' he murmured, under the flow of tap water. He rinsed his mouth. 'Sure,' he said.

Nothing from her in the bed.

'Women are funny,' he said to himself in the mirror.

She lay in the bed.

'Sure,' he said. He gargled with some antiseptic, spat it down the drain. 'You'll be all right in the morning,' he said.

Not a word from her.

'We'll get the car fixed.'

She didn't say anything.

'Be morning before you know it.' He was screwing caps on things now, putting freshener on his face. 'And the car fixed tomorrow, maybe, at the very latest the next day. You won't mind another night here, will you?'

She didn't answer.

'*Will* you?' he asked.

No reply.

The light blinked out under the bathroom door.

'Marie?'

He opened the door.

'Asleep?'

She lay with eyes wide, breasts moving up and down.

'Asleep,' he said. 'Well, good night, lady.'

He climbed into his bed. 'Tired,' he said.

No reply.

'Tired,' he said.

The wind tossed the lights outside; the room was oblong and black and he was in his bed dozing already.

She lay, eyes wide, the watch ticking on her wrist, breasts moving up and down.

It was a fine day coming through the Tropic of Cancer. The automobile pushed along the turning road leaving the jungle country behind, heading for the United States, roaring between the green hills, taking every turn, leaving behind a faint vanishing trail of exhaust smoke. And inside the shiny automobile sat Joseph with his pink, healthy face and his Panama hat, and a little camera cradled on his lap as he drove; a swathe of black silk pinned around the left upper arm of his tan coat. He watched the country slide by and absent-mindedly made a gesture to the seat beside him, and stopped.

He broke into a little sheepish smile and turned once more to the window of his car, humming a tuneless tune, his right hand slowly reaching over to touch the seat beside him . . .

Which was empty.

The Lake

The wave shut me off from the world, from the birds in the sky, the children on the beach, my mother on the shore. There was a moment of green silence. Then the wave gave me back to the sky, the sand, the children yelling. I came out of the lake and the world was waiting for me, having hardly moved since I went away.

I ran up on the beach.

Mama swabbed me with a furry towel. 'Stand there and dry,' she said.

I stood there, watching the sun take away the water beads on my arms. I replaced them with goose-pimples.

'My, there's a wind,' said Mama. 'Put on your sweater.'

'Wait'll I watch my goose-bumps,' I said.

'Harold,' said Mama.

I put the sweater on and watched the waves come up and fall down on the beach. But not clumsily. On purpose, with a green sort of elegance. Even a drunken man could not collapse with such elegance as those waves.

It was September. In the last days when things are getting sad for no reason. The beach was so long and lonely with only about six people on it. The kids quit bouncing the ball because somehow the wind made them sad, too, whistling the way it did, and the kids sat down and felt autumn come along the endless shore.

All of the hot-dog stands were boarded up with strips of golden planking, sealing in all the mustard, onion, meat odours of the long, joyful summer. It was like nailing summer into a series of coffins. One by one the places slammed their covers down, padlocked their doors, and the wind came and touched the sand, blowing away all of the million footprints of July and August. It got so that now, in September, there was nothing but the mark of my rubber tennis shoes and Donald and Delaus Arnold's feet, down by the water curve.

Sand blew up in curtains on the sidewalks, and the merry-go-round was hidden with canvas, all of the horses frozen in mid-air on their brass poles, showing teeth, galloping on. With only the wind for music, slipping through canvas.

I stood there. Everyone else was in school. I was not. Tomorrow I would be on my way west across the United States on a train. Mom and I had come to the beach for one last brief moment.

There was something about the loneliness that made me want to get away by myself. 'Mama, I want to run up the beach aways,' I said.

'All right, but hurry back, and don't go near the water.'

I ran. Sand spun under me and the wind lifted me. You know how it is, running, arms out so you feel veils from your fingers, caused by wind. Like wings.

Mama withdrew into the distance, sitting. Soon she was only a brown speck and I was all alone.

Being alone is a newness to a twelve-year-old child. He is so used to people about. The only way he can be alone is in his mind. There are so many real people around, telling children what and how to do, that a boy has to run off down a beach, even if it's only in his head, to get by himself in his own world.

So now I was really alone.

I went down to the water and let it cool up to my stomach. Always before, with the crowd, I hadn't dared to look, to come to this spot and search around in the water and call a certain name. But now –

Water is like a magician. Sawing you in half. It feels as if you were cut in two, part of you, the lower part, sugar, melting, dissolving away. Cool water, and once in a while a very elegantly stumbling wave that fell with a flourish of lace.

I called her name. A dozen times I called it.

'Tally! Tally! Oh, Tally!'

You really expect answers to your calling when you are young. You feel that whatever you may think can be real. And sometimes maybe that is not so wrong.

I thought of Tally, swimming out into the water last May, with her pigtails trailing, blond. She went laughing, and the sun was on her small twelve-year-old shoulders. I thought of the water settling quiet, of the life guard leaping into it, of Tally's mother screaming, and of how Tally never came out . . .

The life guard tried to persuade her to come out, but she did not. He came back with only bits of water-weed in his big-knuckled fingers, and Tally was gone. She would not sit across from me at school any longer, or chase indoor balls on the brick streets on summer nights. She had gone too far out, and the lake would not let her return.

And now in the lonely autumn when the sky was huge and the water was huge and the beach was so very long, I had come down for the last time, alone.

I called her name again and again. Tally, oh, Tally!

The wind blew so very softly over my ears, the way wind blows over the mouths of sea-shells to set them whispering. The water rose, embraced my chest, then my knees, up and down, one way and another, sucking under my heels.

'Tally! Come back, Tally!'

I was only twelve. But I know how much I loved her. It was that love that comes before all significance of body and morals. It was that love that is no more bad than wind and sea and sand lying side by side for ever. It was made of all the warm long days together at the beach, and the humming quiet days of droning education at the school. All the long autumn days of the years past when I had carried her books home from school.

Tally!

I called her name for the last time. I shivered. I felt water on my face and did not know how it got there. The waves had not splashed that high.

Turning, I retreated to the sand and stood there for half an hour, hoping for one glimpse, one sign, one little bit of Tally to remember. Then, I knelt and built a sand castle, shaping it fine, building it as Tally and I had often built so many of them. But this time I only built half of it. Then I got up.

'Tally, if you hear me, come in and build the rest.'

I walked off towards that far-away speck that was Mama. The water came in, blended the sand castle circle by circle, mashing it down little by little into the original smoothness.

Silently, I walked along the shore.

Far away, a merry-go-round jangled faintly, but it was only the wind.

The next day, I went away on the train.

A train has a poor memory; it soon puts all behind it. It forgets the cornlands of Illinois, the rivers of childhood, the bridges, the lakes, the valleys, the cottages, the hurts and the joys. It spreads them out behind and they drop back of a horizon.

I lengthened my bones, put flesh on them, changed my young mind for an older one, threw away clothes as they no longer fitted, shifted from grammar to high school, to college. And then there was a young woman in Sacramento. I knew her for a time, and we were married. By the time I was twenty-two, I had almost forgotten what the East was like.

Margaret suggested that our delayed honeymoon be taken back in that direction.

Like a memory, a train works both ways. A train can bring rushing back all those things you left behind so many years before.

Lake Bluff, population 10,000, came up over the sky. Margaret looked so handsome in her fine new clothes. She watched me as I felt my old world gather me back into its living. She held my arm as the train slid into Bluff Station and our baggage was escorted out.

So many years, and the things they do to people's faces and bodies. When we walked through the town together I saw no one I recognized. There were faces with echoes in them. Echoes of hikes on ravine trails. Faces with small laughter in them from closed grammar schools and swinging on metal-linked swings and going up and down on teeter-totters. But I didn't speak. I walked and looked and filled up inside with all those memories, like leaves stacked for autumn burning.

We stayed on two weeks in all, revisiting all the places together. The days were happy. I thought I loved Margaret well. At least I thought I did.

It was on one of the last days that we walked down by the shore. It was not quite as late in the year as that day so many years before, but the first evidences of desertion were coming upon the beach. People were thinning out, several of the hot-dog stands had been shuttered and nailed, and the wind, as always, waited there to sing for us.

I almost saw Mama sitting on the sand as she used to sit. I had that feeling again of wanting to be alone. But I could not force myself to speak of this to Margaret. I only held on to her and waited.

It got late in the day. Most of the children had gone home and only a few men and women remained basking in the windy sun.

The life-guard boat pulled up on the shore. The life guard stepped out of it, slowly, with something in his arms.

I froze there. I held my breath and I felt small, only

twelve years old, very little, very infinitesimal and afraid.
The wind howled. I could not see Margaret. I could see
only the beach, the life guard slowly emerging from the
boat with a grey sack in his hands, not very heavy, and
his face almost as grey and lined.

'Stay here, Margaret,' I said. I don't know why I said it.

'But, why?'

'Just stay here, that's all –'

I walked slowly down the sand to where the life guard
stood. He looked at me.

'What is it?' I asked.

The life guard kept looking at me for a long time and
he couldn't speak. He put the grey sack on the sand, and
water whispered wet upon it and went back.

'What is it?' I insisted.

'Strange,' said the life guard, quietly.

I waited.

'Strange,' he said, softly. 'Strangest thing I ever saw.
She's been dead a long time.'

I repeated his words.

He nodded. 'Ten years, I'd say. There haven't been any
children drowned here since 1933, but we found all of them
before a few hours had passed. All except one, I remember.
This body here, why it must be ten years in the water. It's
not – pleasant.'

I stared at the grey sack in his arms. 'Open it,' I said. I
don't know why I said it. The wind was louder.

He fumbled with the sack.

'Hurry, man, open it!' I cried.

'I better not do that,' he said. Then perhaps he saw
the way my face must have looked. 'She was such a
little girl –'

He opened it only part way. That was enough.

The beach was deserted. There was only the sky and
the wind and the water and the autumn coming on lonely.
I looked down at her there.

I said something over and over. A name. The life guard looked at me. 'Where did you find her?' I asked.

'Down the beach, that way, in the shallow water. It's a long, long time for her, isn't it?'

I shook my head.

'Yes, it is. Oh God, yes it is.'

I thought: people grow. I have grown. But she has not changed. She is still small. She is still young. Death does not permit growth or change. She still has golden hair. She will be for ever young and I will love her for ever, oh God, I will love her for ever.

The life guard tied up the sack again.

Down the beach, a few moments later, I walked by myself. I stopped, and looked down at something. This is where the life guard found her, I said to myself.

There, at the water's edge, lay a sand castle, only half-built. Just like Tally and I used to build them. She half and I half.

I looked at it. I knelt beside the sand castle and saw the small prints of feet coming in from the lake and going back out to the lake again and not returning.

Then – I knew.

'I'll help you finish it,' I said.

I did. I built the rest of it up very slowly, then I arose and turned away and walked off, so as not to watch it crumble in the waves, as all things crumble.

I walked back up the beach to where a strange woman named Margaret was waiting for me, smiling . . .

The Crowd

Mr Spallner put his hands over his face.

There was the feeling of movement in space, the beautifully tortured scream, the impact and tumbling of the car with wall, through wall, over and down like a toy, and him hurled out of it. Then – silence.

The crowd came running. Faintly, where he lay, he heard them running. He could tell their ages and their sizes by the sound of their numerous feet over the summer grass and on the lined pavement, and over the asphalt street, and picking through the cluttered bricks to where his car hung half into the night sky, still spinning its wheels with a senseless centrifuge.

Where the crowd came from he didn't know. He struggled to remain aware and then the crowd faces hemmed in upon him, hung over him like the large glowing leaves of down-bent trees. They were a ring of shifting, compressing, changing faces over him, looking down, looking down, reading the time of his life or death by his face, making his face into a moon-dial, where the moon cast a shadow from his nose out upon his cheek to tell the time of breathing or not breathing any more ever.

How swiftly a crowd comes, he thought, like the iris of an eye compressing in out of nowhere.

A siren. A police voice. Movement. Blood trickled from his lips and he was being moved into an ambulance. Someone said, 'Is he dead?' And someone else said, 'No, he's not dead.' And a third person said, 'He won't die, he's not going to die.' And he saw the faces of the crowd beyond him in the night, and he knew by their expressions that he wouldn't die. And that was strange. He saw a man's face, thin, bright, pale; the man swallowed and bit his lips, very sick. There was a small woman, too, with red hair and too much red on her cheeks and lips. And a little boy with a freckled face. Others' faces. An old man with a wrinkled upper lip, an old woman, with a mole upon her chin. They had all come from – where? Houses, cars, alleys, from the immediate and the accident-shocked world. Out of alleys and out of hotels and out of streetcars and seemingly out of nothing they came.

The crowd looked at him and he looked back at them and did not like them at all. There was a vast wrongness to them. He couldn't put his finger on it. They were far worse than this machine-made thing that happened to him now.

The ambulance doors slammed. Through the windows he saw the crowd looking in, looking in. That crowd that always came so fast, so strangely fast, to form a circle, to peer down, to probe, to gawk, to question, to point, to disturb, to spoil the privacy of a man's agony by their frank curiosity.

The ambulance drove off. He sank back and their faces still stared into his face, even with his eyes shut.

The car wheels spun in his mind for days. One wheel, four wheels, spinning, spinning, and whirring, around and around.

He knew it was wrong. Something wrong with the wheels and the whole accident and the running of feet and the curiosity. The crowd faces mixed and spun into the wild rotation of the wheels.

He awoke.

Sunlight, a hospital room, a hand taking his pulse.

'How do you feel?' asked the doctor.

The wheels faded away. Mr Spallner looked around.

'Fine – I guess.'

He tried to find words. About the accident. 'Doctor?'

'Yes?'

'That crowd – was it last night?'

'Two days ago. You've been here since Thursday. You're all right, though. You're doing fine. Don't try and get up.'

'That crowd. Something about wheels, too. Do accidents make people, well, a – little off?'

'Temporarily, sometimes.'

He lay staring up at the doctor. 'Does it hurt your time sense?'

'Panic sometimes does.'

'Makes a minute seem like an hour, or maybe an hour seem like a minute?'

'Yes.'

'Let me tell you then.' He felt the bed under him, the sunlight on his face. 'You'll think I'm crazy. I was driving too fast, I know, I'm sorry now. I jumped the kerb and hit that wall. I was hurt and numb, I know, but I still remember things. Mostly – the crowd.' He waited a moment and then decided to go on, for he suddenly knew what it was that bothered him. 'The crowd got there too quickly. Thirty seconds after the smash they were all standing over me and staring at me . . . it's not right they should run that fast, so late at night . . .'

'You only think it was thirty seconds,' said the doctor. 'It was probably three or four minutes. Your senses –'

'Yeah, I know – my senses, the accident. But I was conscious! I remember one thing that puts it all together and makes it funny, God, so damned funny. The wheels of my car, upside down. The wheels were still spinning when the crowd got there!'

The doctor smiled.

The man in bed went on. 'I'm positive! The wheels were spinning and spinning fast – the front wheels! Wheels don't spin very long, friction cuts them down. And these were really spinning!'

'You're confused,' said the doctor.

'I'm not confused. That street was empty. Not a soul in

sight. And then the accident and the wheels still spinning and all those faces over me, quick, in no time. And the way they looked down at me, I *knew* I wouldn't die . . .'

'Simple shock,' said the doctor, walking away into the sunlight.

They released him from the hospital two weeks later. He rode home in a taxi. People had come to visit him during his two weeks on his back, and to all of them he had told his story, the accident, the spinning wheels, the crowd. They had all laughed with him concerning it, and passed it off.

He leaned forward and tapped on the taxi window.

'What's wrong?'

The cabbie looked back. 'Sorry, boss. This is one helluva town to drive in. Got an accident up ahead. Want me to detour?'

'Yes. No, no! Wait. Go ahead. Let's – let's take a look.'

The cab moved forward, honking.

'Funny damn thing,' said the cabbie. 'Hey, *you*! Get that fleatrap out the way!' Quieter, 'Funny thing – more damn people. Nosy people.'

Mr Spallner looked down and watched his fingers tremble on his knee. 'You noticed that, too?'

'Sure,' said the cabbie. 'All the time. There's always a crowd. You'd think it was their own mother got killed.'

'They come running awfully fast,' said the man in the back of the cab.

'Same way with a fire or an explosion. Nobody around. Boom. Lotsa people around. I dunno.'

'Ever seen an accident – at night?'

The cabbie nodded. 'Sure. Don't make no difference. There's always a crowd.'

The wreck came in view. A body lay on the pavement. You knew there was a body even if you couldn't see it. Because of the crowd. The crowd with its back towards him as he sat in the rear of the cab. With its back towards him. He opened the window and almost started to yell. But he didn't have the nerve. If he yelled they might turn around.

And he was afraid to see their faces.

'I seem to have a penchant for accidents,' he said, in his office. It was late afternoon. His friend sat across the desk from him, listening. 'I got out of the hospital this morning and first thing on the way home, we detoured around a wreck.'

'Things run in cycles,' said Morgan.

'Let me tell you about my accident.'

'I've heard it. Heard it all.'

'But it was funny, you must admit.'

'I must admit. Now how about a drink?'

They talked on for half an hour or more. All the while they talked, at the back of Spallner's brain a small watch ticked, a watch that never needed winding. It was the memory of a few little things. Wheels and faces.

At about five-thirty there was a hard metal noise in the street. Morgan nodded and looked out and down. 'What'd I tell you? Cycles. A truck and a cream-coloured Cadillac. Yes, yes.'

Spallner walked to the window. He was very cold and as he stood there, he looked at his watch, at the small minute hand. One two three four five seconds – people running – eight nine ten eleven twelve – from all over, people came running – fifteen sixteen seventeen eighteen seconds – more people, more cars, more horns blowing. Curiously distant, Spallner looked upon the scene as an explosion in reverse, the fragments of the detonation sucked back to the point of impulsion. Nineteen, twenty, twenty-one seconds and the crowd was there. Spallner made a gesture down at them, wordless.

The crowd had gathered so fast.

He saw a woman's body a moment before the crowd swallowed it up.

Morgan said, 'You look lousy. Here. Finish your drink.'

'I'm all right, I'm all right. Let me alone. I'm all right. Can you see those people? Can you see any of them? I wish we could see them closer.'

Morgan cried out, 'Where in hell are you going?'

Spallner was out the door, Morgan after him, and down the stairs, as rapidly as possible. 'Come along, and hurry.'

'Take it easy, you're not a well man!'

They walked out on to the street. Spallner pushed his way forward. He thought he saw a red-haired woman with too much red colour on her cheeks and lips.

'There!' He turned wildly to Morgan. 'Did you see her?'

'See *who*?'

'Damn it; she's gone. The crowd closed in!'

The crowd was all around, breathing and looking and shuffling and mixing and mumbling and getting in the way when he tried to shove through. Evidently the red-haired woman had seen him coming and run off.

He saw another familiar face! A little freckled boy. But there are many freckled boys in the world. And, anyway, it was no use, before Spallner reached him, this little boy ran away and vanished among the people.

'Is she dead?' a voice asked. 'Is she dead?'

'She's dying,' someone else replied. 'She'll be dead before the ambulance arrives. They shouldn't have moved her. They shouldn't have moved her. They shouldn't have moved her.'

All the crowd faces – familiar, yet unfamiliar, bending over, looking down, looking down.

'Hey, mister, stop pushing.'

'Who you shovin', buddy?'

Spallner came back out, and Morgan caught hold of him

before he fell. 'You damned fool. You're still sick. Why in hell d'you have to come down here?' Morgan demanded.

'I don't know, I really don't. They moved her, Morgan, someone moved her. You should never move a traffic victim. It kills them. It kills them.'

'Yeah. That's the way with people. The idiots.'

Spallner arranged the newspaper clippings carefully.

Morgan looked at them. 'What's the idea? Ever since your accident you think every traffic scramble is part of you. What are these?'

'Clippings of motor-car crackups, and photos. Look at them. Not at the cars,' said Spallner, 'but at the crowds around the cars.' He pointed. 'Here. Compare this photo of a wreck in the Wilshire District with one in Westwood. No resemblance. But now take this Westwood picture and align it with one taken in the Westwood District ten years ago.' Again he motioned. 'This woman is in both pictures.'

'Coincidence. The woman happened to be there once in 1936, and again in 1946.'

'A coincidence once, maybe. But twelve times over a period of ten years, when the accidents occurred as much as three miles from one another, no. Here.' He dealt out a dozen photographs. 'She's in *all* of these!'

'Maybe she's perverted.'

'She's more than that. How does she *happen* to be there so quickly after each accident? And why does she wear the same clothes in pictures taken over a period of a decade?'

'I'll be damned, so she does.'

'And, last of all, why was she standing over *me* the night of my accident, two weeks ago?'

They had a drink. Morgan went over the files. 'What'd you do, hire a clipping service while you were in the hospital to go back through the newspapers for you?'

Spallner nodded. Morgan sipped his drink. It was getting late. The street lights were coming on in the streets below the office. 'What does all this add up to?'

'I don't know,' said Spallner, 'except that there's a universal law about accidents. *Crowds gather.* They always gather. And like you and me, people have wondered year after year, why they gathered so quickly, and how? I know the answer. Here it is!'

He flung the clippings down. 'It frightens me.'

'These people – mightn't they be thrill-hunters, perverted sensationalists with a carnal lust for blood and morbidity?'

Spallner shrugged. 'Does that explain their being at all the accidents? Notice, they stick to certain territories. A Brentwood accident will bring out one group. A Huntington Park another. But there's a norm for faces, a certain percentage appear at each wreck.'

Morgan said, 'They're not *all* the same faces, are they?'

'Naturally not. Accidents draw normal people, too, in the course of time. But these, I find, are always the *first* ones there.'

'Who are they? What do they want? You keep hinting and never telling. Good Lord, you must have some idea. You've scared yourself and now you've got me jumping.'

'I've tried getting to them, but someone always trips me up, I'm always too late. They slip into the crowd and vanish. The crowd seems to offer protection to some of its members. They see me coming.'

'Sounds like some sort of clique.'

'They have one thing in common, they always show up together. At a fire or an explosion or on the sidelines of a war, at any public demonstration of this thing called death. Vultures, hyenas or saints, I don't know which they are, I just don't know. But I'm going to the police with it, this evening. It's gone on long enough. One of them shifted that woman's body today. They shouldn't have touched her. It killed her.'

He placed the clippings in a briefcase. Morgan got up and slipped into his coat. Spallner clicked the briefcase shut. 'Or, I just happened to think . . .'

'What?'

'Maybe they *wanted* her dead.'

'Why?'

'Who knows? Come along.'

'Sorry. It's late. See you tomorrow. Luck.' They went out together. 'Give my regards to the cops. Think they'll believe you?'

'Oh, they'll believe me all right. Good night.'

Spallner took it slow driving downtown.

'I want to get there,' he told himself, 'alive.'

He was rather shocked, but not surprised, somehow, when the truck came rolling out of an alley straight at him. He was just congratulating himself on his keen sense of observation and talking out what he would say to the police in his mind, when the truck smashed into his car. It wasn't really his car, that was the disheartening thing about it. In a preoccupied mood he was tossed first this way and then that way, while he thought, what a shame, Morgan has gone and lent me his extra car for a few days until my other car is fixed, and now here I go again. The windshield hammered back into his face. He was forced back and forth in several lightning jerks. Then all motion stopped and all noise stopped and only pain filled him up.

He heard their feet running and running and running. He fumbled with the car door. It clicked. He fell out upon the pavement drunkenly and lay, ear to the asphalt, listening to them coming. It was like a great rainstorm, with many drops, heavy and light and medium, touching the earth. He waited a few seconds and listened to their coming and their arrival. Then, weakly, expectantly, he rolled his head up and looked.

The crowd was there.

He could smell their breaths, the mingled odours of many people sucking and sucking on the air a man needs to live by. They crowded and jostled and súcked and sucked all the air up from around his gasping face until he tried to tell them to move back, they were making him live in a vacuum. His head was bleeding very badly. He tried to move and he realized something was wrong with his spine. He hadn't felt much at the impact, but his spine was hurt. He didn't dare move.

He couldn't speak. Opening his mouth, nothing came out but a gagging.

Someone said, 'Give me a hand. We'll roll him over and lift him into a more comfortable position.'

Spallner's brain burst apart.

No! Don't move me!

'We'll move him,' said the voice, casually.

You idiots, you'll kill me, don't!

But he could not say any of this out loud. He could only think it.

Hands took hold of him. They started to lift him. He cried out and nausea choked him up. They straightened him out into a ramrod of agony. Two men did it. One of them was thin, bright, pale, alert, a young man. The other man was very old and had a wrinkled upper lip.

He had seen their faces before.

A familiar voice said, 'Is – is he dead?'

Another voice, a memorable voice, responded, 'No. Not yet. But he will be dead before the ambulance arrives.'

It was all a very silly, mad plot. Like every accident. He squealed hysterically at the solid wall of faces. They were all around him, these judges and jurors with the faces he had seen before. Through his pain he counted their faces.

The freckled boy. The old man with the wrinkled upper lip.

The red-haired, red-cheeked woman. An old woman with a mole on her chin.

I know what you're here for, he thought. You're here just as you're at all accidents. To make certain the right ones live and the right ones die. That's why you lifted me. You knew it would kill. You knew I'd live if you left me alone.

And that's the way it's been since time began, when crowds gather. You murder much easier, this way. Your alibi is very simple; you didn't know it was dangerous to move a hurt man. You didn't mean to hurt him.

He looked at them, above him, and he was curious as a man under deep water looking up at people on a bridge. Who are you? Where do you come from and how do you get here so soon? You're the crowd that's always in the way, using up good air that a dying man's lungs are in need of, using up space he should be using to lie in, alone. Tramping on people to make sure they die, that's you. I know *all* of you.

It was like a polite monologue. They said nothing. Faces. The old man. The red-haired woman.

Someone picked up his briefcase. 'Whose is this?'

It's mine! It's evidence against all of you!

Eyes, inverted over him. Shiny eyes under tousled hair or under hats.

Faces.

Somewhere – a siren. The ambulance was coming.

But, looking at the faces, the construction, the cast, the form of the faces, Spallner saw it was too late. He read it in their faces. They *knew*.

He tried to speak. A little bit got out:

'It – looks like I'll – be joining up with you. I – guess I'll be a member of your – group – now.'

He closed his eyes, then waited for the coroner.

Jack-in-the-Box

He looked through the cold morning windows with the Jack-in-the-Box in his hands, prying the rusted lid. But no matter how he struggled, the Jack would not jump to the light with a cry, or slap its velvet mittens on the air, or bob in a dozen directions with a wild and painted smile. Crushed under the lid, in its jail, it stayed crammed tight coil on coil. With your ear to the box you felt pressure beneath, the fear and panic of the trapped toy. It was like holding someone's heart in your hand. Edwin could not tell if the box pulsed or if his own blood beat against the lid.

He threw the box down and looked to the window. Outside the window the trees surrounded the house which surrounded Edwin. He could not see beyond the trees. If he tried to find another World beyond them, the trees wove themselves thick with the wind, to still his curiosity, to stop his eyes.

'Edwin!' Behind him, Mother's waiting, nervous breath as she drank her breakfast coffee. 'Stop staring. Come eat.'

'No,' he whispered.

'What?' A stiffened rustle. She must have turned. 'Which is more important, breakfast or that window?'

'The window . . .' he whispered and sent his gaze running the paths and trails he had tried for thirteen years. Was it true that the trees flowed on ten thousand miles to nothingness? He could not say. His sight returned defeated, to the lawn, the steps, his hands trembling on the pane.

He turned to eat his tasteless apricots, alone with his mother in the vast and echoing breakfast room. Five thousand mornings at this table, this window, and no movement beyond the trees.

The two of them ate silently.

She was the pale woman that no one but the birds saw in old country houses in fourth-floor cupola windows, each morning at six, each afternoon at four, each evening at nine, and also passing by one minute after midnight, there she would be, in her tower, silent and white, high and alone and quiet. It was like passing a deserted greenhouse in which one last wild white blossom lifted its head to the moonlight.

And her child, Edwin, was the thistle that one breath of wind might unpod in a season of thistles. His hair was silken and his eyes were of a constant blue and feverish temperature. He had a haunted look, as if he slept poorly. He might fly apart like a packet of ladyfinger firecrackers if a certain door slammed.

His mother began to talk, slowly and with great caution, then more rapidly, and then angrily, and then almost spitting at him.

'Why must you disobey every morning? I don't like your staring from the window, do you hear? What do you want? Do you want to see them?' she cried, her fingers twitching. She was blazingly lovely, like an angry white flower. 'Do you want to see the Beasts that run down paths and crush people like strawberries?'

Yes, he thought, I'd like to see the Beasts, horrible as they are.

'Do you want to go out there?' she cried. 'Like your father did before you were born, and be killed as he was killed, struck down by one of those Terrors on the road, would you like that?'

'No . . .'

'Isn't it enough they murdered your father? Why should you even think of those Beasts?' She motioned towards the forest. 'Well, if you really want to die that much, go ahead!'

She quieted, but her fingers kept opening and closing

on the tablecloth. 'Edwin, Edwin, your father built every part of this World, it was beautiful for him, it should be for you. There's nothing, nothing, beyond those trees but death; I won't have you near it! This is the World. There's no other worth bothering with.'

He nodded miserably.

'Smile now, and finish your toast,' she said.

He ate slowly, with the window reflected in secret on his silver spoon.

'Mom . . . ?' He couldn't say it. 'What's . . . dying? You talk about it. Is it a feeling?'

'To those who must live on after someone else, a bad feeling, yes.' She stood up suddenly. 'You're late for school! Run!'

He kissed her as he grabbed his books. ''Bye!'

'Say hello to Teacher!'

He fled from her like a bullet from a gun. Up endless staircases, through passages, halls, past windows that poured down dark gallery panels like white waterfalls. Up, up through the layer-cake Worlds with the thick frostings of Oriental rug between, and bright candles on top.

From the highest stair he gazed down through four intervals of Universe.

Lowlands of kitchen, dining room, parlour. Two Middle Countries of music, games, pictures, and locked, forbidden rooms. And here – he whirled – the Highlands of picnics, adventure, and learning. Here he roamed, idled, or sat singing lonely child songs on the winding journey to school.

This, then, was the Universe. Father (or God, as Mother often called him) had raised its mountains of wallpapered plaster long ago. This was Father-God's creation, in which stars blazed at the flick of a switch. And the sun was Mother, and Mother was the sun, about which all the Worlds swung, turning. And Edwin, a small dark meteor, spun up around through the dark carpets and shimmering tapestries of space. You saw him rise to vanish on vast comet staircases, on hikes and explorations.

Sometimes he and Mother picnicked in the Highlands, spread cool snow linens on red-tufted, Persian lawns, on crimson meadows in a rarefied plateau at the summit of the Worlds where flaking portraits of sallow strangers looked meanly down on their eating and their revels. They drew water from silver taps in hidden tiled niches, smashed the tumblers on hearthstones, shrieking. Played hide-and-seek in enchanted Upper Countries, in unknown, wild, and hidden lands, where she found him rolled like a mummy in a velvet window drape or under sheeted furniture like a rare plant protected from some wind. Once, lost, he wandered for hours in insane foothills of dust and echoes, where the hooks and hangers in closets were hung only with night. But she found him and carried him weeping down through the levelling Universe to the Parlour where dust motes, exact and familiar, fell in showers of sparks on the sunlit air.

He ran up a stair.

Here he knocked a thousand thousand doors, all locked and forbidden. Here Picasso ladies and Dali gentlemen screamed silently from canvas asylums, their gold eyes burning when he dawdled.

'Those Things live *out there*,' his mother had said, pointing to the Dali-Picasso families.

Now running quickly past, he stuck out his tongue at them.

He stopped running.

One of the forbidden doors stood open.

Sunlight slanted warm through it, exciting him.

Beyond the door, a spiral stair screwed around up in sun and silence.

He stood, gasping. Year after year he had tried the doors that were always found locked. What would happen now if he shoved this one full open and climbed the stair? Was some Monster hiding at the top?

'Hello!'

His voice leapt up around the spiralled sunlight. 'Hello . . .' whispered a faint, far lazy echo, high, high, and gone.

He moved through the door.

'Please, please, don't hurt me,' he whispered to the high sunlit place.

He climbed, pausing with each step to wait for his punishment, eyes shut like a penitent. Faster now, he leapt around and around and up until his knees ached and his breath fountained in and out and his head banged like a bell and at last he reached the terrible summit of the climb and stood in an open, sun-drenched tower.

The sun struck his eyes a blow. Never, never so much sun! He stumbled to the iron rail.

'It's there!' His mouth opened from one direction to another. 'It's there!' He ran in a circle. 'There!'

He stood above the sombre tree barrier. For the first time he stood high over the windy chestnuts and elms and as far as he could see was green grass, green trees, and white ribbons on which beetles ran, and the other half of the world was blue and endless, with the sun lost and dropping away in an incredible deep blue room so vast he felt himself fall with it, screamed, and clutched the tower ledge, and beyond the trees, beyond the white ribbons where the beetles ran he saw things like fingers sticking up, but he saw no Dali-Picasso terrors, he saw only some small red-and-white-and-blue handkerchiefs fluttering high on great white poles.

He was suddenly sick; he was sick again.

Turning, he almost fell flat down the stairs.

He slammed the forbidden door, fell against it.

'You'll go blind.' He crushed his hands to his eyes. 'You shouldn't have seen, you shouldn't, you shouldn't!'

He fell to his knees, he lay on the floor twisted tight,

covered up. He need wait but a moment – the blindness
would come.

Five minutes later he stood at an ordinary Highlands
window, looking out at his own familiar Garden World.

He saw once more the elms and hickory trees and
the stone wall, and that forest which he had taken to
be an endless wall itself, beyond which lay nothing but
nightmare nothingness, mist, rain, and eternal night. Now
it was certain, the Universe did not end with the forest.
There were other worlds than those contained in Highland
or Lowland.

He tried the forbidden door again. Locked.

Had he really gone up? Had he really discovered those
half-green, half-blue vastnesses? Had God seen him?
Edwin trembled. God. God, who smoked mysterious
black pipes and wielded magical walking sticks. God who
might be watching even now!

Edwin murmured, touching his cold face.

'I can still see. Thank you, thank you. I can *still* see!'

At nine-thirty, half an hour late, he rapped on the school
door.

'Good morning, Teacher!'

The door swung open. Teacher waited in her tall grey,
thick-clothed monk's robe, the cowl hiding her face. She
wore her usual silver spectacles. Her grey-gloved hands
beckoned.

'You're late.'

Beyond her the land of books burned in bright colours from the hearth. There were walls bricked with
encyclopaedias, and a fireplace in which you could stand
without bumping your head. A log blazed fiercely.

The door closed, and there was a warm quiet. Here
was the desk, where God had once sat; he'd walked this
carpet, stuffing his pipe with rich tobacco, and scowled
out that vast, stained-glass window. The room smelled

of God, rubbed wood, tobacco, leather, and silver coins. Here, Teacher's voice sang like a solemn harp, telling of God, the old days, and the World when it had shaken with God's determination, trembled at his wit, when the World was a building under God's hand, a blueprint, a cry, and timber rising. God's fingerprints still lay like half-melted snowflakes on a dozen sharpened pencils in a locked glass display. They must never never be touched lest they melt away for ever.

Here, here in the Highlands, to the soft sound of Teacher's voice running on, Edwin learned what was expected of him and his body. He was to grow into a Presence, he must fit the odours and the trumpet voice of God. He must some day stand tall and burning with pale fire at his high window to shout dust off the beams of the Worlds; he must be God Himself! Nothing must prevent it. Not the sky or the trees or the Things beyond the trees.

Teacher moved like a vapour in the room.

'Why are you late, Edwin?'

'I don't know.'

'I'll ask you again. Edwin, why are you late?'

'One – one of the forbidden doors was open . . .'

He heard the hiss of Teacher's breath. He saw her slowly slide back and sink into the large hand-carved chair, swallowed by darkness, her glasses flashing light before they vanished. He felt her looking out at him from shadow and her voice was numbed and so like a voice he heard at night, his own voice crying just before he woke from some nightmare. 'Which door? Where?' she said. 'Oh, it must be locked!'

'The door by the Dali-Picasso people,' he said, in panic. He and Teacher had always been friends. Was that finished now? Had he spoiled things? 'I climbed the stair. I had to, I had to! I'm sorry, I'm sorry. Please, don't tell Mother!'

Teacher sat lost in the hollow chair, in the hollow cowl. Her glasses made faint firefly glitters in the well where she moved alone. 'And what did you *see* up there?' she murmured.

'A big blue room!'

'Did you?'

'And a green one, and ribbons with bugs running on them, but I didn't, I didn't stay long, I swear, I swear!'

'Green room, ribbons, yes, ribbons, and the little bugs running along them, yes,' she said, and her voice made him sad.

He reached out for her hand, but it fell away to her lap and groped back, in darkness, to her breast. 'I came right down, I locked the door, I won't go look again, ever!' he cried.

Her voice was so faint he could hardly hear what she said. 'But now you've seen, and you'll want to see more, and you'll always be curious now.' The cowl moved slowly back and forth. Its deepness turned towards him, questioning. 'Did you – *like* what you saw?'

'I was scared. It was big.'

'Big, yes, too big. Large, large, so large, Edwin. Not like *our* world. Big, large, uncertain. Oh, why did you do this? You knew it was wrong!'

The fire bloomed and withered on the hearth while she waited for his answer and finally when he could not answer she said, as if her lips were barely moving, 'Is it your Mother?'

'I don't know!'

'Is she nervous, is she mean, does she snap at you, does she hold too tight, do you want time alone, is that it, is that it, is that it?'

'Yes, yes!' he sobbed, wildly.

'Is that why you ran off, she demands all your time, all your thoughts?' Lost and sad, her voice. 'Tell me . . .'

His hands had gone sticky with tears. 'Yes!' He bit his fingers and the backs of his hands. 'Yes!' It was wrong to admit such things, but he didn't have to say them now, she said them, she said them, and all he must do is agree, shake his head, bite his knuckles, cry out between sobs.

Teacher was a million years old.

'We learn,' she said, wearily. Rousing from her chair, she moved with a slow swaying of grey robes to the desk where her gloved hand searched a long time to find pen and paper. 'We learn, oh God, but slowly, and with pain, we learn. We think we do right, but all the time, all the time, we kill the Plan . . .' She hissed her breath, jerked her head up suddenly. The cowl looked completely empty, shivering.

She wrote words on the paper.

'Give this to your mother. It tells her you must have two full hours every afternoon to yourself, to prowl where you wish. Anywhere. Except *out there*. Are you listening, child?'

'Yes.' He dried his face. 'But –'

'Go on.'

'Did Mother lie to me about *out there*, and the Beasts?'

'Look at me,' she said. 'I've been your friend, I've never beaten you, as your mother sometimes must. We're both here to help you understand and grow so you won't be destroyed as God was.'

She arose, and in rising, turned the cowl such a way that colour from the hearth washed over her face. Swiftly, the firelight erased her many wrinkles.

Edwin gasped. His heart gave a jolting thump. 'The fire!'

Teacher froze.

'The fire!' Edwin looked at the fire and back to her face. The cowl jerked away from his gaze, the face vanished in the deep well, gone. 'Your face,' said Edwin numbly. 'You look like Mother!'

She moved swiftly to the books, seized one down. She talked to the shelves in her high, singing, monotonous voice. 'Women look alike, you know that! Forget it!

Here, here!' And she brought him the book. 'Read the first chapter! Read the diary!'

Edwin took the book but did not feel its weight in his hands. The fire rumbled and sucked itself brilliantly up the flue as he began to read and as he read Teacher sank back down and settled and quieted and the more he read the more the grey cowl nodded and became serene, the hidden face like a clapper solemn in its bell. Firelight ignited the gold animal lettering of the shelved books as he read and spoke the words but was really thinking of these books from which pages had been razored, and clipped, certain lines erased, certain pictures torn, the leather jaws of some books glued tight, others like mad dogs, muzzled in hard bronze straps to keep him away. All this he thought while his lips moved through the fire-quiet:

'In the Beginning was God, Who created the Universe, and the Worlds within the Universe, the Continents within the Worlds and the Lands within the Continents, and shaped from His mind and hand His loving wife and a child who in time would be God Himself . . .'

Teacher nodded slowly. The fire fell softly away to slumbering coals. Edwin read on.

Down the banister, breathless, he slid into the Parlour. 'Mom, Mom!'

She lay in a plump maroon chair, breathless, as if she, too, had run a great way.

'Mom, Mom, you're soaking wet!'

'Am I?' she said, as if it was his fault she'd been rushing about. 'So I am, so I am.' She took a deep breath and sighed. Then she took his hands and kissed each one. She looked at him steadily, her eyes dilating. 'Well now, listen here, I've a surprise! Do you know what's coming tomorrow? You can't guess! Your birthday!'

'But it's only been ten months!'

'Tomorrow it is! Do us wonders, I say. And anything I *say* is so is *really* so, my dear.'

She laughed.

'And we open another secret room?' He was dazed.

'The fourteenth room, yes! Fifteenth room next year, sixteenth, seventeenth, and so on and on till your twenty-first birthday, Edwin! Then, oh, then we'll open up the triple-locked doors to the most important room and you'll be Man of the House, Father, God, Ruler of the Universe!'

'Hey,' he said. And, 'Hey!' He tossed his books straight up in the air. They exploded like a great burst of doves, whistling. He laughed. She laughed. Their laughter flew and fell with the books. He ran to scream down the banister again.

At the bottom of the stairs, she waited, arms wide, to catch him.

Edwin lay on his moonlit bed and his fingers pried at the Jack-in-the-Box, but the lid stayed shut; he turned it in his hands, blindly, but did not look down at it. Tomorrow, his birthday – but why? Was he *that* good? No. Why then, should the birthday come so soon? Well, simply because things had gotten, what word could you use? Nervous? Yes, things had begun to shimmer by day as well as by night. He saw the white tremor, the moonlight sifting down and down of an invisible snow in his mother's face. It would take yet another of his birthdays to quiet her again.

'My birthdays,' he said to the ceiling, 'will come quicker from now on. I know, I know. Mom laughs so loud, so much, and her eyes are funny . . .'

Would Teacher be invited to the party? No. Mother and Teacher had never met. 'Why not?' 'Because,' said Mom.

'Don't you *want* to meet Mom, Teacher?' 'Someday,' said Teacher, faintly, blowing off like cobwebs in the hall. 'Someday . . .'

And where did Teacher go at night? Did she drift through all those secret mountain countries high up near the moon where the chandeliers were skinned blind with dust, or did she wander out beyond the trees that lay beyond the trees that lay beyond the trees? No, hardly that!

He twisted the toy in his sweating hands. Last year, when things began to tremble and quiver, hadn't Mother advanced his birthday several months, too? Yes, oh, yes, yes.

Think of something else. God. God building cold midnight cellar, sun-baked attic, and all miracles between. Think of the hour of his death, crushed by some monstrous beetle beyond the wall. Oh, how the Worlds must have rocked with His passing!

Edwin moved the Jack-in the-Box to his face, whispered against the lid. 'Hello! Hello! Hello, hello . . .'

No answer save the sprung-tight coiled-in tension there. I'll get you out, thought Edwin. Just wait, just wait. It may hurt, but there's only one way. Here, here . . .

And he moved from bed to window and leaned far out, looking down to the marbled walk in the moonlight. He raised the box high, felt the sweat trickle from his armpit, felt his fingers clench, felt his arm jerk. He flung the box out, shouting. The box tumbled in the cold air, down. It took a long time to strike the marble pavement.

Edwin bent still further over, gasping.

'Well?' he cried. 'Well?' and again, 'You there!' and 'You!' The echoes faded. The box lay in the forest shadows. He could not see if the crash had broken it wide. He could not see if the Jack had risen, smiling, from its hideous jail or if it bobbed upon the wind now this way, that, this way, that, its silver bells jingling softly. He listened. He stood by the window for an hour staring, listening, and at last went back to bed.

Morning. Bright voices moved near and far, in and out the Kitchen World and Edwin opened his eyes.

Whose voices, now whose could they be? Some of God's workmen? The Dali people? But Mother hated them; no. The voices faded in a humming roar. Silence. And from a great distance, a running, running grew louder and still louder until the door burst open.

'Happy birthday!'

They danced, they ate frosted cookies, they bit lemon ices, they drank pink wines, and there stood his name on a snow-powdered cake as Mother chorded the piano into an avalanche of sound and opened her mouth to sing, then whirled to seize him away to more strawberries, more wines, more laughter that shook chandeliers into trembling rain. Then, a silver key flourished, they raced to unlock the fourteenth forbidden door.

'Ready? Hold on!'

The door whispered into the wall.

'Oh,' said Edwin.

For, disappointingly enough, this fourteenth room was nothing at all but a dusty dull-brown closet. It promised nothing as had the rooms given him on other anniversaries! His sixth birthday present, now, had been the schoolroom in the Highlands. On his seventh birthday he had opened the playroom in the Lowlands. Eighth, the music room; ninth, the miraculous hell-fired kitchen! Tenth was the room where phonographs hissed in a continuous exhalation of ghosts singing on a gentle wind. Eleventh was the vast green diamond room of the Garden with a carpet that had to be cut instead of swept!

'Oh, don't be disappointed; move!' Mother, laughing, pushed him in the closet. 'Wait till you see how magical! Shut the door!'

She thrust a red button flush with the wall.

Edwin shrieked. 'No!'

For the room was quivering, working, like a mouth that held them in iron jaws; the room moved, the wall slid away below.

'Oh, hush now, darling,' she said. The door drifted down through the floor, and a long, insanely vacant wall slithered by like an endlessly rustling snake to bring another door and another door with it that did not stop but travelled on while Edwin screamed and clutched his mother's waist. The room whined and cleared its throat somewhere; the trembling ceased, the room stood still. Edwin stared at a strange new door and heard his mother say go on, open it, there, now, there. And the new door gaped upon still further mystery. Edwin blinked.

'The Highlands! This is the Highlands! How did we get here? Where's the Parlour, Mom, where's the Parlour?'

She fetched him out through the door. 'We jumped straight up, and we flew. Once a week, you'll fly to school instead of running the long way around!'

He still could not move, but only stood looking at the mystery of Land exchanged for Land, of Country replaced by higher and further Country.

'Oh, Mother, Mother . . .' he said.

It was a sweet long time in the deep grass of the garden where they idled most deliciously, sipped huge cupfuls of apple cider with their elbows on crimson silk cushions, their shoes kicked off, their toes bedded in sour dandelions, sweet clover. Mother jumped twice when she heard Monsters roar beyond the forest. Edwin kissed her cheek. 'It's all right,' he said, 'I'll protect you.'

'I know you will,' she said, but she turned to gaze at the pattern of trees, as if any moment the chaos out there might smash the forest with a blow and stamp its Titan's foot down and grind them to dust.

Late in the long blue afternoon, they saw a chromium bird thing fly through a bright rift in the trees, high and roaring. They ran for the Parlour, heads bent as before a green storm of lightning and rain, feeling the sound pour blinding showers to drench them.

Crackle, crackle – the birthday burnt away to cellophane nothingness. At sunset, in the dim soft Parlour Country, Mother inhaled champagne with her tiny seedling nostrils and her pale summer-rose mouth, then, drowsy wild, herded Edwin off to his room and shut him in.

He undressed in slow-pantomimed wonder, thinking, this year, next year, and which room two years, three years, from today? What about the Beasts, the Monsters? And being mashed and God killed? What was killed? What was Death? Was Death a feeling? Did God enjoy it so much he never came back? Was Death a journey then?

In the hall, on her way downstairs, Mother dropped a champagne bottle. Edwin heard and was cold, for the thought that jumped through his head was, that's how Mother'd sound. If she fell, if she broke, you'd find a million fragments in the morning. Bright crystal and clear wine on the parquet flooring, that's all you'd see at dawn.

Morning was the smell of vines and grapes and moss in his room, a smell of shadowed coolness. Downstairs, breakfast was in all probability, at this instant, manifesting itself in a fingersnap on the wintry tables.

Edwin got up to wash and dress and wait, feeling fine. Now things would be fresh and new for at least a month. Today, like all days, there'd be breakfast, school, lunch, songs in the music room, an hour or two at the electrical games, then – tea in the Outlands, on the luminous grass. Then up to school again for a late hour or so, where he and Teacher might prowl the censored library together and he'd puzzle with words and thoughts about that World *out there* that had been censored from his eyes.

He had forgotten Teacher's note. Now, he must give it to Mother.

He opened the door. The hall was empty. Down through the deeps of Worlds, a soft mist floated, through a silence

which no footsteps broke; the hills were quiet; the silver
fonts did not pulse in the first sunlight, and the banister,
coiling up from the mists, was a prehistoric monster peering
into his room. He pulled away from this creature, looking
to find Mother, like a white boat, drifted by the dawn tides
and vapours below.

She was not there. He hurried down through the hushed
lands, calling, 'Mother!'

He found her in the Parlour, collapsed on the floor in her
shiny green-gold party dress, a champagne goblet in one
hand, the carpet littered with broken glass.

She was obviously asleep, so he sat at the magical
breakfast table. He blinked at the empty white cloth
and the gleaming plates. There was no food. All his life
wondrous foods had awaited him here. But not today.

'Mother, wake up!' He ran to her. 'Shall I go to school?
Where's the food? Wake up!'

He ran up the stairs.

The Highlands were cold and shadowed, and the white
glass suns no longer glowed from the ceilings in this
day of sullen fog. Down dark corridors, through dim
continents of silence, Edwin rushed. He rapped and
rapped at the school door. It drifted in, whining, by
itself.

The school lay empty and dark. No fire roared on the
hearth to toss shadows on the beamed ceiling. There was
not a crackle or a whisper.

'Teacher?'

He poised in the centre of the flat, cold room.

'Teacher!' he screamed.

He slashed the drapes aside; a faint shaft of sunlight fell
through the stained glass.

Edwin gestured. He commanded the fire to explode
like a popcorn kernel on the hearth. He commanded it
to bloom to life! He shut his eyes to give Teacher time to

appear. He opened his eyes and was stupefied at what he saw on her desk.

Neatly folded was the grey cowl and robe, atop which gleamed her silver spectacles, and one grey glove. He touched them. One grey glove was gone. A piece of greasy cosmetic chalk lay on the robe. Testing it, he made dark lines on his hands.

He drew back, staring at Teacher's empty robe, the glasses, the greasy chalk. His hand touched a knob of a door which had always been locked. The door swung slowly wide. He looked into a small brown closet.

'Teacher!'

He ran in, the door crashed shut, he pressed a red button. The room sank down, and with it sank a slow mortal coldness. The World was silent, quiet, and cool. Teacher gone and Mother – sleeping. Down fell the room, with him in its iron jaws.

Machinery clashed. A door slid open. Edwin ran out.

The Parlour!

Behind was not a door, but a tall oak panel from which he had emerged.

Mother lay uncaring, asleep. Folded under her, barely showing as he rolled her over, was one of Teacher's soft grey gloves.

He stood near her, holding the incredible glove, for a long time. Finally, he began to whimper.

He fled back up to the Highlands. The hearth was cold, the room empty. He waited. Teacher did not come. He ran down again to the solemn Lowlands, commanded the table to fill with steaming dishes! Nothing happened. He sat by his mother, talking and pleading with her and touching her, and her hands were cold.

The clock ticked and the light changed in the sky and still she did not move, and he was hungry and the silent dust dropped down on the air through all the Worlds. He thought of Teacher and knew that if she was in none of the hills and mountains above, then there was only one place she could be. She had wandered, by error, into the Outlands, lost until someone found her. And so he must go out, call after her, bring her back to wake Mother, or she would lie here for ever with the dust falling in the great darkened spaces.

Through the kitchen, out back, he found late afternoon sun and the Beasts hooting faintly beyond the rim of the World. He clung to the garden wall, not daring to let go, and in the shadows, at a distance, saw the shattered box he had flung from the window. Freckles of sunlight quivered on the broken lid and touched tremblingly over and over the face of the Jack jumped out and sprawled with its arms overhead in an eternal gesture of freedom. The doll smiled and did not smile, smiled and did not smile, as the sun winked on the mouth, and Edwin stood, hypnotized, above and beyond it. The doll opened its arms towards the path that led off between the secret trees, the forbidden path smeared with oily droppings of the Beasts. But the path lay silent and the sun warmed Edwin and he heard the wind blow softly in the trees. At last, he let go of the garden wall.

'Teacher?'

He edged along the path a few feet.

'Teacher!'

His shoes slipped on the animal droppings and he stared far down the motionless tunnel, blindly. The path moved under, the trees moved over him.

'Teacher!'

He walked slowly but steadily. He turned. Behind him lay his World and its very new silence. It was diminished, it was small! How strange to see it less than it had been. It had always and for ever seemed so large. He felt his heart stop. He stepped back. But then, afraid of that silence in the World, he turned to face the forest path ahead.

Everything before him was new. Odours filled his

nostrils, colours, odd shapes, incredible sizes filled his eyes.

If I run beyond the trees I'll die, he thought, for that's what Mother said. You'll die, you'll die.

But what's dying? Another room? A blue room, a green room, far larger than all the rooms that ever were! But where's the key? There, far ahead, a great half-open iron door, a wrought-iron gate. Beyond, a room as large as the sky, all coloured green with trees and grass! Oh, Mother, Teacher . . .

He rushed, stumbled, fell, got up, ran again, his numb legs under him were left behind as he fell down and down the side of a hill, the path gone, wailing, crying, and then not wailing or crying any more, but making new sounds. He reached the great rusted, screaming iron gate, leapt through, the Universe dwindled behind, he did not look back at his old Worlds, but ran as they withered and vanished.

The policeman stood at the kerb, looking down the street. 'These kids. I'll never be able to figure them.'

'How's that?' asked the pedestrian.

The policeman thought it over and frowned. 'Couple seconds ago a little kid ran by. He was laughing and crying, crying and laughing, both. He was jumping up and down and touching things. Things like lamp-posts, the telephone poles, fire hydrants, dogs, people. Things like sidewalks, fences, gates, cars, plateglass windows, barber poles. Hell, he even grabbed hold and looked at me, and looked at the sky; you should have seen the tears, and all the time he kept yelling and yelling something funny.'

'What did he yell?' asked the pedestrian.

'He kept yelling, "I'm dead, I'm dead, I'm glad I'm dead, I'm dead, I'm dead, I'm glad I'm dead, I'm dead, I'm dead, it's *good* to be dead!"' The policeman scratched his chin slowly. 'One of them new kid games, I guess.'

The Man Upstairs

He remembered how carefully and expertly Grandmother would fondle the cold cut guts of the chicken and withdraw the marvels therein; the wet shining loops of meat-smelling intestine, the muscled lump of heart, the gizzard with the collection of seeds in it. How neatly and nicely Grandma would slit the chicken and push her fat little hand in to deprive it of its medals. These would be segregated, some in pans of water, others in paper to be thrown to the dog later, perhaps. And then the ritual of taxidermy, stuffing the bird with watered, seasoned bread, and performing surgery with a swift, bright needle, stitch after pulled-tight stitch.

This was one of the prime thrills of Douglas's eleven-year-old life span.

Altogether, he counted twenty knives in the various squeaking drawers of the magic kitchen table from which Grandma, a kindly, gentle-faced, white-haired old witch, drew paraphernalia for her miracles.

Douglas was to be quiet. He could stand across the table from Grandma, his freckled nose tucked over the edge, watching, but any loose boy-talk might interfere with the spell. It was a wonder when Grandma brandished silver shakers over the bird, supposedly sprinkling showers of mummy-dust and pulverized Indian bones, muttering mystical verses under her toothless breath.

'Grammy,' said Douglas at last, breaking the silence. 'Am I like that inside?' He pointed at the chicken.

'Yes,' said Grandma. 'A little more orderly and presentable, but just about the same . . .'

'And more *of* it!' added Douglas, proud of his guts.

'Yes,' said Grandma. 'More of it.'

'Grandpa has lots more'n me. His sticks out in front so he can rest his elbows on it.'

Grandma laughed and shook her head.

Douglas said, 'And Lucie Williams, down the street, she . . .'

'Hush, child!' cried Grandma.

'But she's got . . .'

'Never you mind what she's got! That's different.'

'But why is *she* different?'

'A darning-needle dragonfly is coming by someday and will sew up your mouth,' said Grandma firmly.

Douglas waited, then asked, 'How do you know I've got insides like that, Grandma?'

'Oh, go 'way, now!'

The front doorbell rang.

Through the front-door glass as he ran down the hall, Douglas saw a straw hat. The bell jangled again and again. Douglas opened the door.

'Good morning, child, is the landlady at home?'

Cold grey eyes in a long, smooth, walnut-coloured face gazed upon Douglas. The man was tall, thin, and carried a suitcase, a briefcase, an umbrella under one bent arm, gloves rich and thick and grey on his thin fingers, and wore a horribly new straw hat.

Douglas backed up. 'She's busy.'

'I wish to rent her upstairs room, as advertised.'

'We've got ten boarders, and it's already rented; go away!'

'Douglas!' Grandma was behind him suddenly. 'How do you do?' she said to the stranger. 'Never mind this child.'

Unsmiling, the man stepped stiffly in. Douglas watched them ascend out of sight up the stairs, heard Grandma detailing the conveniences of the upstairs room. Soon she hurried down to pile linens from the linen closet on Douglas and send him scooting up with them.

Douglas paused at the room's threshold. The room was

changed oddly, simply because the stranger had been in it a moment. The straw hat lay brittle and terrible upon the bed, the umbrella leaned stiff against one wall like a dead bat with dark moist wings folded.

Douglas blinked at the umbrella.

The stranger stood in the centre of the changed room, tall, tall.

'Here!' Douglas littered the bed with supplies. 'We eat at noon sharp, and if you're late coming down the soup'll get cold. Grandma fixes it so it will, every time!'

The tall strange man counted out ten new copper pennies and tinkled them in Douglas's blouse pocket. 'We shall be friends,' he said, grimly.

It was funny, the man having nothing but pennies. Lots of them. No silver at all, no dimes, no quarters. Just new copper pennies.

Douglas thanked him glumly. 'I'll drop these in my dime bank when I get them changed into a dime. I got six dollars and fifty cents in dimes all ready for my camp trip in August.'

'I must wash now,' said the tall strange man.

Once, at midnight, Douglas had wakened to hear a storm rumbling outside – the cold hard wind shaking the house, the rain driving against the window. And then a lightning bolt had landed outside the window with a silent, terrific concussion. He remembered that fear of looking about at his room, seeing it strange and awful in the instantaneous light.

So it was, now, in this room. He stood looking up at the stranger. This room was no longer the same, but changed indefinably because this man, quick as a lightning bolt, had shed his light about it. Douglas backed up slowly as the stranger advanced.

The door closed in his face.

*   *   *

The wooden fork went up with mashed potatoes, came down empty. Mr Koberman, for that was his name, had brought the wooden fork and wooden knife and spoon with him when Grandma called lunch.

'Mrs Spaulding,' he had said, quietly, 'my own cutlery; please use it. I will have lunch today, but from tomorrow on, only breakfast and supper.'

Grandma bustled in and out, bearing steaming tureens of soup and beans and mashed potatoes to impress her new boarder, while Douglas sat rattling his silverware on his plate, because he had discovered it irritated Mr Koberman.

'I know a trick,' said Douglas. 'Watch.' He picked a fork-tine with his fingernail. He pointed at various sectors of the table, like a magician. Wherever he pointed, the sound of the vibrating fork-tine emerged, like a metal elfin voice. Simply done, of course. He pressed the fork handle on the table-top secretly. The vibration came from the wood like a sounding board. It looked quite magical. 'There, there, and *there*!' exclaimed Douglas, happily plucking the fork again. He pointed at Mr Koberman's soup and the noise came from it.

Mr Koberman's walnut-coloured face became hard and firm and awful. He pushed the soup bowl away violently, his lips twisting. He fell back in his chair.

Grandma appeared. 'Why, what's wrong, Mr Koberman?'

'I cannot eat this soup.'

'Why?'

'Because I am full and can eat no more. Thank you.'

Mr Koberman left the room, glaring.

'What did you do, just then?' asked Grandma at Douglas, sharply.

'Nothing. Grandma, why does he eat with *wooden* spoons?'

'Yours not to question! When do you go back to school, anyway?'

'Seven weeks.'

'Oh, my land!' said Grandma.

Mr Koberman worked nights. Each morning at eight he arrived mysteriously home, devoured a very small breakfast, and then slept soundlessly in his room all through the dreaming hot daytime, until the huge supper with all the other boarders at night.

Mr Koberman's sleeping habits made it necessary for Douglas to be quiet. This was unbearable. So, whenever Grandma visited down the street, Douglas stomped up and down stairs beating a drum, bouncing golf balls, or just screaming for three minutes outside Mr Koberman's door, or flushing the toilet seven times in succession.

Mr Koberman never moved. His room was silent, dark. He did not complain. There was no sound. He slept on and on. It was very strange.

Douglas felt a pure white flame of hatred burn inside himself with a steady, unflickering beauty. Now that room was Koberman Land. Once it had been flowery bright when Miss Sadlowe lived there. Now it was stark, bare, cold, clean, everything in its place, alien and brittle.

Douglas climbed upstairs on the fourth morning.

Halfway to the second floor was a large sun-filled window, framed by six-inch panes of orange, purple, blue, red and burgundy glass. In the enchanted early mornings when the sun fell through to strike the landing and slide down the stair banister, Douglas stood entranced at this window peering at the world through the multicoloured panes.

Now a blue world, a blue sky, blue people, blue streetcars and blue trotting dogs.

He shifted panes. Now – an amber world! Two lemonish women glided by, resembling the daughters of Fu Manchu! Douglas giggled. This pane made even the sunlight more purely golden.

It was eight A.M. Mr Koberman strolled by below, on the sidewalk, returning from his night's work, his cane looped over his elbow, straw hat glued to his head with patent oil.

Douglas shifted panes again. Mr Koberman was a red man walking through a red world with red trees and red flowers and – something else.

Something about – Mr Koberman.

Douglas squinted.

The red glass *did* things to Mr Koberman. His face, his suit, his hands. The clothes seemed to melt away. Douglas almost believed, for one terrible instant, that he could see *inside* Mr Koberman. And what he saw made him lean wildly against the small red pane, blinking.

Mr Koberman glanced up just then, saw Douglas, and raised his cane-umbrella angrily, as if to strike. He ran swiftly across the red lawn to the front door.

'Young man!' he cried, running up the stairs. 'What were you doing?'

'Just looking,' said Douglas, numbly.

'That's all, is it?' cried Mr Koberman.

'Yes, sir. I look through all the glasses. All kinds of worlds. Blue ones, red ones, yellow ones. All different.'

'All kinds of worlds, is it!' Mr Koberman glanced at the little panes of glass, his face pale. He got hold of himself. He wiped his face with a handkerchief and pretended to laugh. 'Yes. All kinds of worlds. All different.' He walked to the door of his room. 'Go right ahead; play,' he said.

The door closed. The hall was empty. Mr Koberman had gone in.

Douglas shrugged and found a new pane.

'Oh, everything's violet!'

Half an hour later, while playing in his sandbox behind the house, Douglas heard the crash and the shattering tinkle. He leaped up.

A moment later, Grandma appeared on the back porch, the old razor strop trembling in her hand.

'Douglas! I told you time and time again never fling your basketball against the house! Oh, I could just cry!'

'I been sitting right here,' he protested.

'Come see what you've done, you nasty boy!'

The great coloured window panes lay shattered in a rainbow chaos on the upstairs landing. His basketball lay in the ruins.

Before he could even begin telling his innocence, Douglas was struck a dozen stinging blows upon his rump. Wherever he landed, screaming, the razor strop struck again.

Later, hiding his mind in the sandpile like an ostrich, Douglas nursed his dreadful pains. He knew who'd thrown that basketball. A man with a straw hat and a stiff umbrella and a cold, grey room. Yeah, yeah, yeah. He dribbled tears. Just wait. Just *wait*.

He heard Grandma sweeping up the broken glass. She brought it out and threw it in the trash bin. Blue, pink, yellow meteors of glass dropped brightly down.

When she was gone, Douglas dragged himself, whimpering, over to save out three pieces of the incredible glass. Mr Koberman disliked the coloured windows. These – he clinked them in his fingers – would be worth saving.

Grandfather arrived from his newspaper office each night, shortly ahead of the other boarders, at five o'clock. When a slow, heavy tread filled the hall, and a thick, mahogany cane thumped in the cane-rack, Douglas ran to embrace the large stomach and sit on Grandpa's knee while he read the evening paper.

'Hi, Grampa!'

'Hello, down there!'

'Grandma cut chickens again today. It's fun watching,' said Douglas.

Grandpa kept reading. 'That's twice this week, chickens.

She's the chickenist woman. You like to watch her cut 'em, eh? Cold-blooded little pepper! Ha!'

'I'm just curious.'

'You are,' rumbled Grandpa, scowling. 'Remember that day when that young lady was killed at the rail station? You just walked over and looked at her, blood and all.' He laughed. 'Queer duck. Stay that way. Fear nothing, ever in your life. I guess you get it from your father, him being a military man and all, and you so close to him before you came here to live last year.' Grandpa returned to his paper.

A long pause. 'Gramps?'

'Yes?'

'What if a man didn't have a heart or lungs or stomach but still walked around, alive?'

'That,' rumbled Gramps, 'would be a miracle.'

'I don't mean a – a miracle. I mean, what if he was all *different* inside? Not like me?'

'Well, he wouldn't be quite human then, would he, boy?'

'Guess not, Gramps. Gramps, you got a heart and lungs?'

Gramps chuckled. 'Well, tell the truth, I don't know. Never seen them. Never had an X-ray, never been to a doctor. Might as well be potato-solid for all I know.'

'Have I got a stomach?'

'You certainly have!' cried Grandma from the parlour entry. ''Cause I feed it! And you've lungs, you scream loud enough to wake the crumblees. And you've dirty hands, go wash them! Dinner's ready. Grandpa, come on. Douglas, git!'

In the rush of boarders streaming downstairs, Grandpa, if he intended questioning Douglas further about the weird conversation, lost his opportunity. If dinner delayed an instant more, Grandma and the potatoes would develop simultaneous lumps.

*　　*　　*

The boarders, laughing and talking at the table – Mr Koberman silent and sullen among them – were silenced when Grandfather cleared his throat. He talked politics a few minutes and then shifted over into the intriguing topic of the recent peculiar deaths in the town.

'It's enough to make an old newspaper editor prick up his ears,' he said, eyeing them all. 'That young Miss Larsson, lived across the ravine, now. Found her dead three days ago for no reason, just funny kinds of tattoos all over her, and a facial expression that would make Dante cringe. And that other young lady, what was her name? Whitely? She disappeared and *never did* come back.'

'Them things happen alla time,' said Mr Britz, the garage mechanic, chewing. 'Ever peek inna Missing Peoples Bureau file? It's *that* long.' He illustrated. 'Can't tell *what* happens to most of 'em.'

'Anyone want more dressing?' Grandma ladled liberal portions from the chicken's interior. Douglas watched, thinking about how that chicken had had two kinds of guts – God-made and Man-made.

Well, how about *three* kinds of guts?

Eh?

Why not?

Conversation continued about the mysterious death of so-and-so, and, oh, yes, remember a week ago, Marion Barsumian died of heart failure, but maybe that didn't connect up? or did it? you're crazy! forget it, why talk about it at the dinner table? So.

'Never can tell,' said Mr Britz. 'Maybe we got a vampire in town.'

Mr Koberman stopped eating.

'In the year 1927?' said Grandma. 'A vampire? Oh, go on, now.'

'Sure,' said Mr Britz. 'Kill 'em with silver bullets. Anything silver for that matter. Vampires *hate* silver. I read it in a book somewhere, once. Sure, I did.'

Douglas looked at Mr Koberman who ate with wooden knives and forks and carried only new copper pennies in his pocket.

'It's poor judgement,' said Grandpa, 'to call anything by a name. We don't know what a hobgoblin or a vampire or a troll is. Could be lots of things. You can't heave them into categories with labels and say they'll act one way or another. That'd be silly. They're people. People who do things. Yes, that's the way to put it: people who do things.'

'Excuse me,' said Mr Koberman, who got up and went out for his evening walk to work.

The stars, the moon, the wind, the clock ticking, and the chiming of the hours into dawn, the sun rising, and here it was another morning, another day, and Mr Koberman coming along the sidewalk from his night's work. Douglas stood off like a small mechanism whirring and watching with carefully microscopic eyes.

At noon, Grandma went to the store to buy groceries.

As was his custom every day when Grandma was gone, Douglas yelled outside Mr Koberman's door for a full three minutes. As usual, there was no response. The silence was horrible.

He ran downstairs, got the pass-key, a silver fork, and the three pieces of coloured glass he had saved from the shattered window. He fitted the key to the lock and swung the door slowly open.

The room was in half light, the shades drawn. Mr Koberman lay atop his bedcovers, in slumber clothes, breathing gently, up and down. He didn't move. His face was motionless.

'Hello, Mr Koberman!'

The colourless walls echoed the man's regular breathing.

'Mr Koberman, hello!'

Bouncing a golf ball, Douglas advanced. He yelled. Still no answer. 'Mr Koberman!'

Bending over Mr Koberman, Douglas pricked the tines of the silver fork in the sleeping man's face.

Mr Koberman winced. He twisted. He groaned bitterly. Response. Good. Swell.

Douglas drew a piece of blue glass from his pocket. Looking through the blue glass fragment he found himself in a blue room, in a blue world different from the world he knew. As different as was the red world. Blue furniture, blue bed, blue ceiling and walls, blue wooden eating utensils atop the blue bureau, and the sullen dark blue of Mr Koberman's face and arms and his blue chest rising, falling. Also . . .

Mr Koberman's eyes were wide, staring at him with a hungry darkness.

Douglas fell back, pulled the blue glass from his eyes.

Mr Koberman's eyes were shut.

Blue glass again – open. Blue glass away – shut. Blue glass again – open. Away – shut. Funny. Douglas experimented, trembling. Through the glass the eyes seemed to peer hungrily, avidly through Mr Koberman's closed lids. Without the blue glass they seemed tightly shut.

But it was the rest of Mr Koberman's body . . .

Mr Koberman's bedclothes dissolved off him. The blue glass had something to do with it. Or perhaps it was the clothes themselves, just being *on* Mr Koberman. Douglas cried out.

He was looking through the wall of Mr Koberman's stomach, right *inside* him!

Mr Koberman was solid.

Or, nearly so, anyway.

There were strange shapes and sizes within him.

Douglas must have stood amazed for five minutes, thinking about the blue worlds, the red worlds, the yellow worlds side by side, living together like glass panes around the big white stair window. Side by side, the coloured panes, the different worlds; Mr Koberman had said so himself.

So this was why the coloured window had been broken.

'Mr Koberman, wake up!'

No answer.

'Mr Koberman, where do you work at night? Mr Koberman, where do you work?'

A little breeze stirred the blue window shade.

'In a red world or a green world or a yellow one, Mr Koberman?'

Over everything was a blue glass silence.

'Wait there,' said Douglas.

He walked down to the kitchen, pulled open the great squeaking drawer and picked out the sharpest, biggest knife.

Very calmly he walked into the hall, climbed back up the stairs again, opened the door to Mr Koberman's room, went in, and closed it, holding the sharp knife in one hand.

Grandma was busy fingering a piecrust into a pan when Douglas entered the kitchen to place something on the table.

'Grandma, what's this?'

She glanced up briefly, over her glasses. 'I don't know.'

It was square, like a box, and elastic. It was bright orange in colour. It had four square tubes, coloured blue, attached to it. It smelled funny.

'Ever see anything like it, Grandma?'

'No.'

'That's what I thought.'

Douglas left it there, went from the kitchen. Five minutes later he returned with something else. 'How about *this*?'

He laid down a bright pink linked chain with a purple triangle at one end.

'Don't bother me,' said Grandma. 'It's only a chain.'

Next time he returned with two hands full. A ring, a square, a triangle, a pyramid, a rectangle, and – other shapes. All of them were pliable, resilient, and looked as if they were made of gelatine. 'This isn't all,' said Douglas, putting them down. 'There's more where this came from.'

Grandma said, 'Yes, yes,' in a far-off tone, very busy.

'You were wrong, Grandma.'

'About what?'

'About all people being the same inside.'

'Stop talking nonsense.'

'Where's my piggy bank?'

'On the mantel, where you left it.'

'Thanks.'

He tromped into the parlour, reached up for his piggy bank.

Grandpa came home from the office at five.

'Grandpa, come upstairs.'

'Sure, son. Why?'

'Something to show you. It's not nice; but it's interesting.' Grandpa chuckled, following his grandson's feet up to Mr Koberman's room.

'Grandma mustn't know about this; she wouldn't like it,' said Douglas. He pushed the door wide open. 'There.'

Grandfather gasped.

Douglas remembered the next few hours all the rest of his life. Standing over Mr Koberman's naked body, the coroner and his assistants. Grandma, downstairs, asking somebody, 'What's going on up there?' and Grandpa saying, shakily, 'I'll take Douglas away on a long vacation so he can forget this whole ghastly affair. Ghastly, ghastly affair!'

Douglas said, 'Why should it be bad? I don't see anything bad. I don't feel bad.'

The coroner shivered and said, 'Koberman's dead, all right.'

His assistant sweated. 'Did you see those *things* in the pans of water and in the wrapping paper?'

'Oh, my God, my God, yes, I saw them.'

'Christ.'

The coroner bent over Mr Koberman's body again. 'This better be kept secret, boys. It wasn't murder. It was a mercy the boy acted. God knows what might have happened if he hadn't.'

'What *was* Koberman? A vampire? A monster?'

'Maybe. I don't know. Something – not human.' The coroner moved his hands deftly over the suture.

Douglas was proud of his work. He'd gone to much trouble. He had watched Grandmother carefully and remembered. Needle and thread and all. All in all, Mr Koberman was as neat a job as any chicken ever popped into hell by Grandma.

'I heard the boy say that Koberman lived even after all those *things* were taken out of him.' The coroner looked at the triangles and chains and pyramids floating in the pans of water. 'Kept on *living*. God.'

'Did the boy say that?'

'He did.'

'Then, what *did* kill Koberman?'

The coroner drew a few strands of sewing thread from their bedding.

'This . . .' he said.

Sunlight blinked coldly off a half-revealed treasure trove; six dollars and seventy cents' worth of silver dimes inside Mr Koberman's chest.

'I think Douglas made a wise investment,' said the coroner, sewing the flesh back up over the 'dressing' quickly.

The Cistern

It was an afternoon of rain, and lamps lighted against
the grey. For a long while the two sisters had been
in the dining-room. One of them, Juliet, embroidered
tablecloths; the younger, Anna, sat quietly on the window
seat, staring out at the dark street and the dark sky.

Anna kept her brow pressed against the pane, but her
lips moved and after reflecting a long moment, she said,
'I never thought of that before.'

'Of what?' asked Juliet.

'It just came to me. There's actually a city under a city.
A dead city, right here, right under our feet.'

Juliet poked her needle in and out the white cloth.
'Come away from the window. That rain's done something
to you.'

'No, really. Didn't you ever think of the cisterns before?
They're all through the town, there's one for every street,
and you can walk in them without bumping your head, and
they go everywhere and finally go down to the sea,' said
Anna, fascinated with the rain on the asphalt pavement
out there and the rain falling from the sky and vanishing
down the gratings at each corner of the distant intersection.
'Wouldn't you like to live in a cistern?'

'I would not!'

'But wouldn't it be fun – I mean, very secret? To live in
the cistern and peek up at people through the slots and see
them and them not see you? Like when you were a child and
played hide-and-seek and nobody found you, and there you
were in their midst all the time, all sheltered and hidden and
warm and excited. I'd like that. That's what it must be like
to live in the cistern.'

Juliet looked slowly up from her work. 'You *are* my sister, aren't you, Anna? You *were* born, weren't you? Sometimes, the way you talk, I think Mother found you under a tree one day and brought you home and planted you in a pot and grew you to this size and there you are, and you'll never change.'

Anna didn't reply, so Juliet went back to her needle. There was no colour in the room; neither of the two sisters added any colour to it. Anna held her head to the window for five minutes. Then she looked way off into the distance and said, 'I guess you'd call it a dream. While I've been here, the last hour, I mean. Thinking. Yes, Juliet, it was a dream.'

Now it was Juliet's turn not to answer.

Anna whispered, 'All this water put me to sleep a while, I guess, and then I began to think about the rain and where it came from and where it went and how it went down those little slots in the kerb, and then I thought about deep under, and suddenly there *they* were. A man . . . and a woman. Down in that cistern, under the road.'

'What would they be doing there?' asked Juliet.

Anna said, 'Must they have a reason?'

'No, not if they're insane, no,' said Juliet. 'In that case no reasons are necessary. There they are in their cistern, and let them stay.'

'But they aren't just in the cistern,' said Anna, knowingly, her head to one side, her eyes moving under the half-down lids. 'No, they're in love, there, these two.'

'For heaven's sake,' said Juliet, 'did love make them crawl down there?'

'No, they've been there for years and years,' said Anna.

'You can't tell me they've been in that cistern for years, living together,' protested Juliet.

'Did I say they were alive?' asked Anna, surprised. 'Oh, but no. They're dead.'

The rain scrambled in wild, pushing pellets down the window. Drops came and joined with others and made streaks.

'Oh,' said Juliet.

'Yes,' said Anna, pleasantly. 'Dead. He's dead and she's dead.' This seemed to satisfy her; it was a nice discovery, and she was proud of it. 'He looked like a very lonely man who never travelled in all his life.'

'How do you know?'

'He looks like the kind of man who never travelled but wanted to. You know by his eyes.'

'You know what he looks like, then?'

'Yes. Very ill and very handsome. You know how it is with a man made handsome by illness? Illness brings out the bones in the face.'

'And he's dead?' asked the older sister.

'For five years.' Anna talked softly, with her eyelids rising and falling, as if she were about to tell a long story and knew it and wanted to work into it slowly, and then faster and then faster, until the very momentum of the story would carry her on, with her eyes wide and her lips parted. But now it was slowly, with only a slight fever to the telling. 'Five years ago this man was walking along a street and he knew he'd been walking the same street on many nights and he'd go on walking it, so he came to a manhole cover, one of those big iron waffles in the centre of the street, and he heard the river rushing under his feet, under the metal cover, rushing towards the sea.' Anna put out her right hand. 'And he bent slowly and lifted up the cistern lid and looked down at the rushing foam and the water, and he thought of someone he wanted to love and couldn't, and then he swung himself on to the iron rungs and walked down them until he was all gone . . .'

'And what about her?' asked Juliet, busy. 'When'd she die?'

'I'm not sure. She's new. She's just dead, now. But she

is dead. Beautifully, beautifully dead.' Anna admired the image she had in her mind. 'It takes death to make a woman really beautiful, and it takes death by drowning to make her most beautiful of all. Then all the stiffness is taken out of her, and her hair hangs up on the water like a drift of smoke.' She nodded her head, amusedly. 'All the schools and etiquettes and teachings in the world can't make a woman move with this dreamy ease, supple and ripply and fine.' Anna tried to show how fine, how ripply, how graceful, with her broad, coarse hand.

'He'd been waiting for her, for five years. But she hadn't known where he was till now. So there they are, and will be, from now on . . . In the rainy season they'll live. But in the dry seasons – that's sometimes months – they'll have long rest periods, they'll lie in little hidden niches, like those Japanese water flowers, all dry and compact and old and quiet.'

Juliet got up and turned on yet another little lamp in the corner of the dining-room. 'I wish you wouldn't talk about it.'

Anna laughed. 'But let me tell you about how it starts, how they come back to life. I've got it all worked out.' She bent forward, held on to her knees, staring at the street and the rain and the cistern mouths. 'There they are, down under, dry and quiet, and up above the sky gets electrical and powdery.' She threw back her dull, greying hair with one hand. 'At first all the upper world is pellets. Then there's lightning and then thunder and the dry season is over, and the little pellets run along the gutters and get big and fall into the drains. They take gum wrappers and theatre tickets with them, and bus transfers!'

'Come away from that window, now.'

Anna made a square with her hands and imagined things. 'I know just what it's like under the pavement, in the big square cistern. It's huge. It's all empty from the weeks with nothing but sunshine. It echoes if you talk. The only sound you can hear standing down there is an auto passing above. Far up above. The whole cistern is like a dry, hollow camel bone in a desert, waiting.'

She lifted her hand, pointing, as if she herself were down in the cistern, waiting. 'Now, a little trickle. It comes down on the floor. It's like something was hurt and bleeding up in the outer world. There's some thunder! Or was it a truck going by?'

She spoke a little more rapidly now, but held her body relaxed against the window, breathing out, and in the next words: 'It seeps down. Then, into all the other hollows come other seepages. Little twines and snakes. Tobacco-stained water. Then it moves. It joins others. It makes snakes and then one big constrictor which rolls along on the flat, papered floor. From everywhere, from the north and south, from other streets, other streams come and they join and make one hissing and shining coil. And the water writhes into those two little dry niches I told you about. It rises slowly around those two, the man and the woman, lying there like Japanese flowers.'

She clasped her hands, slowly, working finger into finger, interlacing.

'The water soaks into them. First, it lifts the woman's hand. In a little move. Her hand's the only live part of her. Then her arm lifts and one foot. And her hair . . .' she touched her own hair as it hung about her shoulders '. . . unloosens and opens out like a flower in the water. Her shut eyelids are blue . . .'

The room got darker, Juliet sewed on, and Anna talked and told all she saw in her mind. She told how the water rose and took the woman with it, unfolding her out and loosening her and standing her full upright in the cistern. 'The water is interested in the woman, and she lets it have its way. After a long time of lying still, she's ready to live again, any life the water wants her to have.'

Somewhere else, the man stood up in the water also. And

Anna told of that, and how the water carried him slowly, drifting, and her, drifting, until they met each other. 'The water opens their eyes. Now they can see but not see each other. They circle, not touching yet.' Anna made a little move of her head, eyes closed. 'They watch each other. They glow with some kind of phosphorus. They smile . . . They – touch hands.'

At last Juliet, stiffening, put down her sewing and stared at her sister, across the grey, rain-silent room.

'Anna!'

'The tide – makes them touch. The tide comes and puts them together. It's a perfect kind of love, with no ego to it, only two bodies, moved by the water, which makes it clean and all right. It's not wicked, this way.'

'It's bad you're saying it!' cried her sister.

'No, it's all right,' insisted Anna, turning for an instant. 'They're not thinking, are they? They're just so deep down and quiet and not caring.'

She took her right hand and held it over her left hand very slowly and gently, quavering and interweaving them. The rainy window, with the pale spring light penetrating, put a movement of light and running water on her fingers, made them seem submerged, fathoms deep in grey water, running one about the other as she finished her little dream:

'Him, tall and quiet, his hands open.' She showed with a gesture how tall and how easy he was in the water. 'Her, small and quiet and relaxed.' She looked at her sister, leaving her hands just that way. 'They're dead, with no place to go, and no one to tell them. So there they are, with nothing applying to them and no worries, very secret and hidden under the earth in the cistern waters. They touch their hands and lips and when they come into a cross-street outlet of the cistern, the tide rushes them together. Then, later . . .' she disengaged her hands . . . 'maybe they travel together, hand in hand, bobbling and floating, down all the streets, doing little crazy upright dances when they're caught in sudden swirls.' She whirled her hands about, a drenching of rain spatted the window. 'And they go down to the sea, all across the town, past cross drain and cross drain, street and street. Genesee Avenue, Crenshaw, Edmond Place, Washington, Motor City, Ocean Side and then the ocean. They go anywhere the water wants them, all over the earth, and come back later to the cistern inlet and float back up under the town, under a dozen tobacco shops and four dozen liquor stores, and six dozen groceries and ten theatres, a rail junction, Highway 101, under the walking feet of thirty thousand people who don't even know or think of the cistern.'

Anna's voice drifted and dreamed and grew quiet again.

'And then – the day passes and the thunder goes away up on the street. The rain stops. The rain season's over. The tunnels drip and stop. The tide goes down.' She seemed disappointed, sad it was over. 'The river runs out to the ocean. The man and woman feel the water leave them slowly to the floor. They settle.' She lowered her hands in little bobblings to her lap, watching them fixedly, longingly. 'Their feet lose the life the water has given them from outside. Now the water lays them down, side by side, and drains away, and the tunnels are drying. And there they lie. Up above, in the world, the sun comes out. There they lie, in the darkness, sleeping, until the next time. Until the next rain.'

Her hands were now upon her lap, palms up and open. 'Nice man, nice woman,' she murmured. She bowed her head over them and shut her eyes tight.

Suddenly Anna sat up and glared at her sister. 'Do you know who the man is?' she shouted, bitterly.

Juliet did not reply; she had watched, stricken, for the past five minutes while this thing went on. Her mouth was twisted and pale. Anna almost screamed:

'The man is Frank, that's who he is! And *I'm* the woman!'

'Anna!'

'Yes, it's Frank, down there!'

'But Frank's been gone for years, and certainly not down there, Anna!'

Now, Anna was talking to nobody, and to everybody, to Juliet, to the window, the wall, the street. 'Poor Frank,' she cried. 'I know that's where he went. He couldn't stay anywhere in the world. His mother spoiled him for all the world! So he saw the cistern and saw how secret and fine it was. Oh, poor Frank. And poor Anna, poor me, with only a sister. Oh, Julie, why didn't I hold on to Frank when he was here? Why didn't I fight to win him from his mother?'

'Stop it, this minute, do you hear, this minute!'

Anna slumped down into the corner, by the window, one hand up on it, and wept silently. A few minutes later she heard her sister say, 'Are you finished?'

'What?'

'If you're done, come help me finish this, I'll be for ever at it.'

Anna raised her head and glided over to her sister. 'What do you want me to do?' she sighed.

'This and this,' said Juliet, showing her.

'All right,' said Anna, and took it and sat by the window looking at the rain, moving her hands with the needle and thread, but watching how dark the street was now, and the room, and how hard it was to see the round metal top of the cistern now – there were just little midnight gleams and glitters out there in the black black late afternoon. Lightning crackled over the sky in a web.

Half an hour passed. Juliet drowsed in her chair across the room, removed her glasses, placed them down with her work and for a moment rested her head back and dozed. Perhaps thirty seconds later she heard the front door open violently, heard the wind come in, heard the footsteps run down the walk, turn, and hurry along the black street.

'What?' asked Juliet, sitting up, fumbling for her glasses. 'Who's there? Anna, did someone come in the door?' She stared at the empty window seat where Anna had been. 'Anna!' she cried. She sprang up and ran out into the hall.

The front door stood open, rain fell through it in a fine mist.

'She's only gone out for a moment,' said Juliet, standing there, trying to peer into the wet blackness. 'She'll be right back. *Won't* you be right back, Anna dear? Anna, answer me, you *will* be right back, won't you, sister?'

Outside, the cistern lid rose and slammed down.

The rain whispered on the street and fell upon the closed lid all the rest of the night.

The Tombstone

Well, first of all there was the long trip, and the dust poking up inside her thin nostrils, and Walter, her Oklahoma husband, swaying his lean carcass in their model-T Ford, so sure of himself it made her want to spit; then they got into this big brick town that was strange as old sin, and hunted up a landlord. The landlord took them to a small room and unlocked the door.

There in the middle of the simple room sat the tombstone.

Leota's eyes got a wise look, and immediately she pretended to gasp, and thoughts skipped through her mind in devilish quickness. Her superstitions were something Walter had never been able to touch or take away from her. She gasped, drew back, and Walter stared at her with his droopy eyelids hanging over his shiny grey eyes.

'No, no,' cried Leota, definitely. 'I'm not moving in any room with any dead man!'

'Leota!' said her husband.

'What do you mean?' wondered the landlord. 'Madam, you don't –'

Leota smiled inwardly. Of course she didn't really believe, but this was her only weapon against her Oklahoma man, so – 'I mean that I won't sleep in no room with no corpse. Get him out of here!'

Walter gazed at the sagging bed wearily, and this gave Leota pleasure, to be able to frustrate him. Yes, indeed, superstitions were handy things. She heard the landlord saying, 'This tombstone is the very finest grey marble. It belongs to Mr Whetmore.'

'The name carved on the stone is WHITE,' observed Leota coldly.

'Certainly. That's the man's name for whom the stone was carved.'

'And is he dead?' asked Leota, waiting.

The landlord nodded.

'There, you *see*!' cried Leota. Walter groaned a groan which meant he was not stirring another inch looking for a room. 'It smells like a cemetery in here,' said Leota, watching Walter's eyes get hot and flinty. The landlord explained:

'Mr Whetmore, the former tenant of this room, was an apprentice marble-cutter, this was his first job, he used to tap on it with a chisel every night from seven until ten.'

'Well –' Leota glanced swiftly around to find Mr Whetmore. 'Where is he? Did he die, too?' She enjoyed this game.

'No, he discouraged himself and quit cutting this stone to work in an envelope factory.'

'Why?'

'He made a mistake.' The landlord tapped the marble lettering. 'WHITE is the name here. Spelled wrong. Should be WHYTE, with a Y instead of an I. Poor Mr Whetmore. Inferiority complex. Gave up at the least little mistake and scuttled off.'

'I'll be damned,' said Walter, shuffling into the room and unpacking the rusty-brown suitcases, his back to Leota. The landlord liked to tell the rest of the story:

'Yes, Mr Whetmore gave up easily. To show you how touchy he was, he'd percolate coffee, mornings, and if he spilled a teaspoonful it was a catastrophe – he'd throw it all away and not drink coffee for days! Think of that! He got very sad when he made errors. If he put his left shoe on first, instead of his right, he'd quit trying and walk barefooted for ten or twelve hours, on cold mornings, even. Or if someone spelled his name wrong

on his letters, he'd replace them in the mailbox marked
NO SUCH PERSON LIVING HERE. Oh, he was a great
one, was Mr Whetmore!'

'That don't paddle us no further up-crick,' pursued Leota
grimly. 'Walter, what're you commencing?'

'Hanging your silk dress in this closet; the red one.'

'Stop hanging, we're not staying.'

The landlord blew out his breath, not understanding
how a woman could grow so dumb. 'I'll explain once
more. Mr Whetmore did his homework here; he hired
a truck which carried this tombstone here one day while
I was out shopping for a turkey at the grocery, and
when I walked back – tap-tap-tap – I heard it all the
way downstairs – Mr Whetmore had started chipping the
marble. And he was so proud I didn't dare complain. But
he was so awful proud he made a spelling mistake and
now he ran off without a word, his rent is paid all the
way till Tuesday, but he didn't want a refund, and now
I've got some truckers with a hoist who'll come up first
thing in the morning. You won't mind sleeping here one
night with it, now will you? Of course not.'

The husband nodded. 'You understand, Leota? Ain't
no dead man under that rug.' He sounded so superior,
she wanted to kick him.

She didn't believe him and she stiffened. She poked a
finger at the landlord. '*You* want your money. And you,
Walter, you want a bed to drop your bones on. Both of
you are lying from the word "go"!'

The Oklahoma man paid the landlord his money tiredly,
with Leota tonguing him. The landlord ignored her as if
she were invisible, said good night and she cried 'Liar!'
after him as he shut the door and left them alone. Her
husband undressed and got into bed and said, 'Don't stand
there staring at the tombstone, turn out the light. We been
travelling four days and I'm bushed.'

Her tight criss-crossed arms began to quiver over her

thin breasts. 'None of the three of us,' she said, nodding at the stone, 'will get any sleep.'

Twenty minutes later, disturbed by the various sounds and movements, the Oklahoma man unveiled his vulture's face from the bed-sheets, blinking stupidly. 'Leota, you still up? I said, a long time ago, for you to switch off the light and come sleep! What are you doing there?'

It was quite evident what she was about. Crawling on rough hands and knees, she placed a jar of fresh-cut red, white and pink geraniums beside the headstone, and another tin-can of new-cut roses at the foot of the imagined grave. A pair of shears lay on the floor, dewy with having snipped flowers in the night outside a moment before.

Now she briskly whisked the colourful linoleum and the worn rug with a midget whisk broom, praying so her husband couldn't hear the words, but just the murmur. When she rose up, she stepped across the grave carefully so as not to defile the buried one, and in crossing the room she skirted far around the spot, saying 'There, that's done,' as she darkened the room and laid herself out on the whining springs which sang in tune with her husband who now asked, 'What in the Lord's name!' and she replied, looking at the dark around her, 'No man's going to rest easy with strangers sleeping right atop him. I made amends with him, flowered his bed so he won't stand around rubbing his bones together late tonight.'

Her husband looked at the place she occupied in the dark, and couldn't think of anything good enough to say, so he just swore, groaned, and sank down into sleeping.

Not half an hour later, she grabbed his elbow and turned him so she could whisper swiftly, fearfully into one of his ears, like a person calling into a cave: 'Walter!' she cried. 'Wake up, wake up!' She intended doing this all night, if need be, to spoil his superior kind of slumber.

He struggled with her. 'What's wrong?'

'Mr White! Mr White! He's starting to haunt us!'

'Oh, go to sleep!'

'I'm not fibbing! Listen to him!'

The Oklahoma man listened. From under the linoleum, sounding about six feet or so down, muffled, came a man's sorrowful talking. Not a word came through clearly, just a sort of sad mourning.

The Oklahoma man sat up in bed. Feeling his movement, Leota hissed, 'You heard, you heard?' excitedly. The Oklahoma man put his feet on the cold linoleum. The voice below changed into a falsetto. Leota began to sob. 'Shut up, so I can hear,' demanded her husband, angrily. Then, in the heart-beating quiet, he bent his ear to the floor and Leota cried, 'Don't tip over the flowers!' and he cried, 'Shut up!' and again listened, tensed. Then he spat out an oath and rolled back under the covers. 'It's only the man downstairs,' he muttered.

'That's what I mean. Mr White!'

'No, not Mr White. We're on the second floor of an apartment house, and we got neighbours down under. Listen.' The falsetto downstairs talked. 'That's the man's wife. She's probably telling him not to look at another man's wife! Both of them probably drunk.'

'You're lying!' insisted Leota. 'Acting brave when you're really trembling fit to shake the bed down. It's a haunt, I tell you, and he's talking in voices, like Gran'ma Hanlon used to do, rising up in her church pew and making queer tongues all mixed like a black man, an Irishman, two women and tree frogs, caught in her craw! That dead man, Mr White, hates us for moving in with him tonight, I tell you! Listen!'

As if to back her up, the voices downstairs talked louder. The Oklahoma man lay on his elbows, shaking his head hopelessly, wanting to laugh, but too tired.

Something crashed.

'He's stirring in his coffin!' shrieked Leota. 'He's mad!

We got to move outa here, Walter, or we'll be found dead tomorrow!'

More crashes, more bangs, more voices. Then, silence. Followed by a movement of feet in the air over their heads.

Leota whimpered. 'He's free of his tomb! Forced his way out and he's tromping the air over our heads!'

By this time, the Oklahoma man had his clothing on. Beside the bed, he put on his boots. 'This building's three floors high,' he said, tucking in his shirt. 'We got neighbours overhead who just come home.' To Leota's weeping he had this to say, 'Come on. I'm taking you upstairs to meet them people. That'll prove who they are. Then we'll walk downstairs to the first floor and talk to that drunkard and his wife. Get up, Leota.'

Someone knocked on the door.

Leota squealed and rolled over and over making a quilted mummy of herself. 'He's in his tomb again, rapping to get out!'

The Oklahoma man switched on the lights and unlocked the door. A very jubilant little man in a dark suit, with wild blue eyes, wrinkles, grey hair and thick glasses danced in.

'Sorry, sorry,' declared the little man. 'I'm Mr Whetmore. I went away. Now I'm back. I've had the most astonishing stroke of luck. Yes, I have. Is my tombstone still here?' He looked at the stone a moment before he saw it. 'Ah, yes, yes, it is! Oh, hello.' He saw Leota peering from many layers of blanket. 'I've some men with a roller-truck, and, if you don't mind, we'll move the tombstone out of here, this very moment. It'll only take a minute.'

The husband laughed with gratitude. 'Glad to get rid of the damned thing. Wheel her out!'

Mr Whetmore directed two brawny workmen into the

room. He was almost breathless with anticipation. 'The most amazing thing. This morning I was lost, beaten, dejected – but a miracle happened.' The tombstone was loaded on to a small coaster truck. 'Just an hour ago, I heard, by chance, of a Mr White who had just died of pneumonia. A Mr White, mind you, who spells his name with an I instead of a Y. I have just contacted his wife, and she is delighted that the stone is all prepared. And Mr White not cold more than sixty minutes, and spelling his name with an I, just think of it. Oh, I'm so happy!'

The tombstone, on its truck, rolled from the room, while Mr Whetmore and the Oklahoma man laughed, shook hands, and Leota watched with suspicion as the commotion came to an end. 'Well, that's now all over,' grinned her husband as he closed the door on Mr Whetmore, and began throwing the canned flowers into the sink and dropping the tin-cans into a waste-basket. In the dark, he climbed into bed again, oblivious to her deep and solemn silence. She said not a word for a long while, but just lay there, alone-feeling. She felt him adjust the blankets with a sigh. 'Now we can sleep. The damn old thing's took away. It's only ten-thirty. Plenty of time for sleep.' How he enjoyed spoiling her fun.

Leota was about to speak when a rapping came from down below again. 'There! There!' she cried, triumphantly, holding her husband. 'There it is again, the noises, like I said. Hear them!'

Her husband knotted his fists and clenched his teeth. 'How many times must I explain? Do I have to kick you in the head to make you understand, woman? Let me alone. There's nothing –'.

'Listen, listen, oh, listen,' she begged in a whisper.

They listened in the square darkness.

A rapping on a door came from downstairs.

A door opened. Muffled and distant and faint, a woman's voice said, sadly, 'Oh, it's you, Mr Whetmore.'

And deep down in the darkness underneath the suddenly shivering bed of Leota and her Oklahoma husband, Mr Whetmore's voice replied: 'Good evening again, Mrs White. Here. I brought the stone.'

The Smiling People

It was the sensation of silence that was the most notable aspect of the house. As Mr Greppin came through the front door the oiled silence of the door opening and swinging closed behind him was like an opening and shutting dream, a thing accomplished on rubber pads, bathed in lubricant, slow and unmaterialistic. The double carpet in the hall, which he himself had so recently laid, gave off no sound from his movements. And when the wind shook the house late of nights there was not a rattle of eave or tremor of loose sash. He had, himself, checked the storm windows. The screen doors were securely hooked with bright new, firm hooks, and the furnace did not knock but sent a silent whisper of warm wind up the throats of the heating system that sighed ever so quietly, moving the cuffs of his trousers as he stood, now, warming himself from the bitter afternoon.

Weighing the silence with the remarkable instruments of pitch and balance in his small ears, he nodded with satisfaction that the silence was so unified and finished. Because there *had* been nights when rats had walked between wall-layers and it had taken baited traps and poisoned food before the walls were mute. Even the grandfather clock had been stilled; its brass pendulum hung frozen and gleaming in its long cedar, glass-fronted coffin.

They were waiting for him in the dining-room.

He listened. They made no sound. Good. Excellent, in fact. They had learned, then, to be silent. You had to teach people, but it was worth while – there was not a stir of a knife or fork from the dining-table. He worked off his thick grey gloves, hung up his cold armour of overcoat and stood there with an expression of urgency and indecisiveness . . . thinking of what had to be done.

Mr Greppin proceeded with familiar certainty and economy of motion into the dining-room, where the four individuals seated at the waiting table did not move or speak a word. The only sound was the merest allowable pad of his shoes on the deep carpet.

His eyes, as usual, instinctively fastened upon the lady heading the table. Passing, he waved a finger near her cheek. She did not blink.

Aunt Rose sat firmly at the head of the table, and if a mote of dust floated lightly down out of the ceiling spaces, did her eye trace its orbit? Did the eye revolve in its shellacked socket, with glassy cold precision? And if the dust mote happened upon the shell of her wet eye did the eye bat? Did the muscles clinch, the lashes close?

No.

Aunt Rose's hand lay on the table like cutlery, rare and fine and old; tarnished. Her bosom was hidden in a salad of fluffy linen. The breasts had not been exhumed for years; either for love or child-suckling. They were mummies wrapped in cerements and put away for all time. Beneath the table her stick legs in high button shoes went up into a sexless pipe of dress. You felt that the legs terminated at the skirt line and from there on she was a department store dummy, all wax and nothingness. You felt that her husband, years ago, must have handled her in just such a way as one handled window mannequins, and she responded with the same chill waxen movements, with as much enthusiasm and response as a mannequin; and the husband, beaten off with no blows and no words, had turned over under the bedding and lain trembling with a feeding passion for many nights and then, finally, silently, taken to evening walks and little places across town, beyond the ravine, where a pink-curtained window glowed with fresher electricity and a young lady answered when he tapped the bell.

So here was Aunt Rose, staring straight at Mr Greppin, and – he choked out a laugh and clapped hands derisively shut – there were the first hints of a dust moustache gathering across her upper lip!

'Good evening, Aunt Rose,' he said, bowing. 'Good evening, Uncle Dimity,' he said, graciously. 'No, not a *word*,' he held up his hand. 'Not a word from any of you.' He bowed again. 'Ah, good evening, cousin Lila, and you, cousin Lester.'

Lila sat upon the left, her hair like golden shavings from a tube of lathed brass. Lester, opposite her, told all directions with *his* hair. They were both young, he fourteen, she sixteen. Uncle Dimity, their father (but 'father' was a nasty word!) sat next to Lila, placed in this secondary niche long long ago because Aunt Rose said the window draught might get his neck if he sat at the head of the table. Ah, Aunt Rose!

Mr Greppin drew the chair under his tight-clothed little rump and put a casual elbow to the linen.

'I've something to say,' he said. 'It's very important. This has gone on for weeks now. It can't go any further. I'm in love. Oh, but I told you that long ago. On the day I made you all smile. Remember?'

The eyes of the four seated people did not blink, the hands did not move.

Greppin became introspective. The day he had made them smile. Two weeks ago it was. He had come home, walked in, looked at them and said, 'I'm to be married!'

They had all whirled with expressions as if someone had just smashed the window.

'You're to be *what*?' cried Aunt Rose.

'To Alice Jane Bellerd!' he had said, stiffening somewhat.

'Congratulations,' said Uncle Dimity. 'I *guess*,' he added, looking at his wife. He cleared his throat. 'But isn't it a little early, son?' He looked at his wife again. 'Yes. Yes, I think it is a little early. I wouldn't advise it yet, not just yet, no.'

'The house is in a terrible way,' said Aunt Rose. 'We won't have it fixed for a year yet.'

'That's what you said last year and the year before,' said Mr Greppin. 'And anyway,' he said, bluntly, 'this is *my* house.'

Aunt Rose's jaw had clamped at that. 'After all these years, for us to be bodily thrown out, why I –'

'You won't be thrown out, don't be idiotic!' said Greppin.

'Now, Rose –' said Uncle Dimity in a pale tone.

Aunt Rose dropped her hands. 'After all I've done –'

In that instant Greppin had known they would *have* to go, all of them. First he would make them silent, then he would make them smile, then, later, he would move them out like luggage. He couldn't bring Alice Jane into a house full of grims such as these, where Aunt Rose followed wherever you went even when she wasn't following you, and the children performed indignities upon you at a glance from their maternal parent, and the father, no better than a third child, carefully rearranged his advice to you on being a bachelor. Greppin stared at them. It was their fault that his loving and living was all wrong. If he did something about them – then his warm, luminous dreams of soft bodies glowing with an anxious perspiration of love might become tangible and near. Then he would have the house for himself and – and Alice Jane. Yes, Alice Jane.

Aunt, Uncle and cousins would have to go. Quickly. If he told them to go, as he had often done, twenty years might pass as Aunt Rose gathered sun-bleached sachets and Edison phonographs. Long before then, Alice Jane herself would be moved and gone.

Greppin looked at them as he picked up the carving-knife.

*   *   *

Greppin's head snapped with tiredness. He flicked his eyes open. Eh? Oh, he had been drowsing, thinking.

All *that* had occurred two weeks ago. Two weeks ago this very night that conversation about marriage, moving, Alice Jane, had come about. Two weeks ago it had been. Two weeks ago he had made them smile.

Now, recovering from his reverie, he smiled around at the silent and motionless figures. They smiled back in a peculiarly pleasing fashion.

'I hate you. You are an old bitch,' he said to Aunt Rose, directly. 'Two weeks ago I wouldn't have dared to say that. Tonight, ah, well –' He lazed his voice, turning. 'Uncle Dimity, let *me* give *you* a little advice, old man –'

He talked small talk, picked up a spoon, pretended to eat peaches from an empty dish. He had already eaten downtown in a restaurant, pork, potatoes, pie, coffee. But now he made dessert-eating motions because he enjoyed this little act. He made as if he were chewing.

'So – tonight you're finally, once and for all, moving out. I've waited two weeks, thinking it all over. In a way, I guess I've kept you here this long because I wanted to keep an eye on you. Once you're gone, I can't be sure –' And here his eyes gleamed with fear. 'You might come prowling around, making noises at night, and I couldn't stand that. I can't ever have noises in this house, not even when Alice moves in . . .'

The double carpet was thick and soundless underfoot, reassuring.

'Alice wants to move in day after tomorrow. We're getting married.'

Aunt Rose winked evilly, doubtfully at him.

'Ah!' he cried, leaping up. Then, staring, he sank down, mouth convulsing. He released the tension in him, laughing. 'Oh, I see. It was a fly.' He watched the fly crawl with slow precision on the ivory cheek of Aunt Rose and dart away. Why did it have to pick that instant to make her eye appear to blink, to doubt? 'Do you doubt I ever will marry, Aunt Rose? Do you think me incapable of marriage, of love and love's duties? Do you think me immature, unable to cope with a woman and her methods? Do you think me a child, only daydreaming? Well!' He calmed himself with an effort, shaking his head. 'Man, man,' he argued to himself, 'it was only a fly. And does a fly make doubt of love, or did you make it into a fly and a wink? Damn it!' He pointed at the four of them. 'I'm going to fix the furnace hotter. In an hour I'll be moving you out of the house once and for all. You comprehend? Good. I see you do.'

Outside, it began to rain, a cold nuzzling downpour that drenched the house. A look of irritation came to Greppin's face. The rain sound was one thing he couldn't stop, the one thing that couldn't be helped. No way to buy new hinges or lubricants or hooks for that. You might tent the housetop with lengths of cloth to soften the sound, mightn't you? That'd be going a bit far. No. No way of preventing the rain sounds.

He wanted silence now, where he had never wanted it in his life so much. Each sound was a fear. So each sound had to be muffled, gotten to and eliminated.

The drum of rain was like the knuckles of an impatient man on a surface. He lapsed again into remembering.

He recalled the rest of it. The rest of that hour on that day two weeks ago when he had made them smile . . .

He had taken up the carving-knife, prepared to cut the bird upon the table. As usual, the family had been gathered, all wearing their solemn, puritanical masks. If the children smiled the smiles were stepped on like nasty bugs by Aunt Rose.

Aunt Rose criticized the angle of Greppin's elbows as he cut the bird. The knife, she made him understand also, was not sharp enough. Oh yes, the sharpness of the knife.

At this point in his memory he stopped, roll-tilted his eyes, and laughed. Dutifully, then, he had crisped the knife on the sharpening rod, and again set upon the fowl. He had severed away much of it in some minutes before he slowly looked up at their solemn, critical faces, like puddings with agate eyes, and after staring at them a moment, as if discovered with a naked woman instead of a naked-limbed partridge, he lifted the knife and yelled hoarsely, 'Why in God's name can't you, *any* of you, ever smile? I'll *make* you smile!'

He raised the knife a number of times like a magician's wand.

And, in a short interval – behold! *all* of them smiled!

He broke that memory in half, crumpled it, balled it, tossed it down. Rising briskly, he went to the hall, down the hall to the kitchen, and from there down the dim stairs into the cellar where he opened the furnace door and built the fire steadily and expertly into wonderful flame.

Walking upstairs again he looked about. He'd have cleaners come and clean the empty house, redecorators pull down the dull drapes and hoist new shimmery banners up. New thick Oriental rugs purchased for the floors would subtly ensure the silence he desired and would need at least for the next month, if not for the entire year.

He put his hands to his ears. What if Alice Jane made noise moving about the house? Some noise, somehow, some place!

Then, he laughed. It was quite a joke. That problem was already solved. He need fear no noise from Alice. It was all absurdly simple. He would have all the pleasure of Alice Jane and none of the dream-destroying distractions and uncomfortables.

There was one other addition needed to the quality of silence. Upon the tops of the doors that the wind sucked shut with a bang at frequent intervals he would install modern air-compression brakes, those kind they have on library doors that hiss gently as their levers seal.

He passed through the dining-room. The figures had not moved from their tableau. Their hands remained affixed in familiar positions, and their indifference to him was not impoliteness.

He climbed the hall stairs to change his clothing, preparatory to the task of moving the family. Taking the links from his fine cuffs he swung his head to one side.

Music.

First, he paid it no mind. Then, slowly, his face lifting to the ceiling, the colour drained from his cheeks.

At the very apex of the house the music sounded, note by note, tone following tone, and it terrified him.

Each tone came like a plucking of one single harp thread. In the complete silence the small sound of it was made larger until it grew out of proportion to itself, gone mad with all this soundlessness to stretch about in.

The door opened in an explosion from his hands, the next thing his feet were trying the stairs to the third level of the house, the banister twisted in a long polished snake under his tightening, relaxing, sliding, reaching-up, pulling hands! The steps went under to be replaced by longer, higher, darker steps. He had started the game at the bottom with a slow stumbling. Now he was running with full impetus and if a wall had suddenly confronted him he'd not have stopped for it until he saw blood on it and fingernail scratches where he tried to pass through.

He felt like a mouse running in a great clear space of a bell. High in the bell sphere the one harp thread hummed. It drew him on, caught him up with an umbilicus of sound, gave his fear sustenance and life, mothered him. Fears passed between mother and groping child. He sought to shear away the connection with his hands, could not. He fell, as if someone'd given a heave on the cord, wriggling.

Another clear threaded tone. And *another*.

'No, keep quiet!' he shouted. 'There can't be noise in *my* house. Not since two weeks ago. I said there'd be no more noise. So there can't be – it's impossible! Keep quiet!'

He burst upwards into the attic.

Relief can be hysteria.

Raindrops, falling from a vent in the roof, struck shattering upon a tall cut-glass Swedish flower vase, with resonant tone.

He destroyed the vase with one violent kick.

Putting on an old shirt and old pair of pants in his room, he chuckled. The music was gone, the vent plugged, the vase in a thousand pieces, the silence again ensured.

There are silences and silences. Each with its own identity. There were summer night silences, which weren't silences at all, but layer on layer of insect chorales and the sound of electric lamps swaying in lonely small orbits on lonely country roads, casting out feeble rings of illumination upon which the night fed – summer night silence which, to be a silence, demanded an indolence and a neglect and an indifference upon the part of the listener. Not a silence at all! And there was a winter silence, but it was an encoffined silence, ready to burst free at the first nod of spring; things had a compressed, a not-for-long feel, the silence made a sound unto itself, the freezing was so complete it made chimes of everything or detonations of a single breath or word you spoke at midnight on the diamond air. No, it was not a silence worthy of the name. There were also other silences. For instance – a silence between two lovers, when there need be no words. Colour came in his cheeks, he shut his eyes. It was a most pleasant silence, even if not complete, because women were always spoiling it by complaining of some little pressure or lack of pressure. He smiled. But with Alice Jane even *that* was eliminated. He had seen to everything. *Everything* was perfect.

Whispering.

He hoped the neighbours hadn't heard him shrieking like a fool.

A faint whispering.

Now, about silences . . . The best silence was one conceived in every aspect by an individual, himself, so that there could be no bursting of crystal bonds, no electric-insect hummings; the human mind could cope with each sound, each emergency, until such a complete silence was achieved that one could hear one's cells adjust in one's hand.

A whispering.

He shook his head. There was no whispering. There could be none in *his* house. Sweat began to seep down his body, his jaw loosened, his eyes were turned free in their sockets.

Whisperings. Low rumours of talk.

'I tell you I'm getting married,' he said, weakly, loosely.

'You're lying,' said the whispers.

His head fell forward on its neck as if hung, chin on chest.

'Her name is Alice Jane –' he mouthed it between soft, wet lips and the words were formless. One of his eyes began to jitter its lid up and down as if blinking out a code to some unseen guest. 'You can't stop me from loving her. I love her –'

Whispering.

He took a blind step forward.

The cuff of his pants leg quivered as he reached the floor grille of the ventilator. A hot rise of air hollowed his cuffs. Whispering.

The furnace.

*   *   *

He was on his way downstairs when someone knocked on the front door.

He leaned against it. 'Who is it?'

'Mr Greppin?'

Greppin drew in his breath. 'Yes?'

'Will you let us in, please?'

'Who is it?'

'The police,' said the man outside.

'What do you want? I'm just sitting down to supper!'

'Just want a talk with you. The neighbours phoned. Said they hadn't seen your aunt and uncle for two weeks. Heard a noise a while ago —'

'I assure you everything is all right.' He forced a laugh.

'Well, then,' continued the voice outside, 'we can talk it over in friendly style if you'll only open the door.'

'I'm sorry,' insisted Greppin. 'I'm tired and hungry, come back tomorrow. I'll talk to you then, if you want.'

'I'll have to *insist*, Mr Greppin.'

They began to beat against the door.

Greppin turned automatically, stiffly, walked down the hall past the cold clock, into the dining-room, without a word. He seated himself without looking at anyone in particular and then he began to talk, slowly at first, then more rapidly.

'Some pests at the door. You'll talk to them, won't you, Aunt Rose? You'll tell them to go away, won't you, we're eating supper? Everyone else go on eating and look pleasant and they'll go away, if they come in. Aunt Rose, you *will* talk to them, won't you? And now that things are happening I have something to tell you.' A few hot tears fell for no reason. He looked at them as they soaked and spread in the white linen, vanishing. 'I don't know anyone named Alice Jane Bellerd. I *never* knew anyone named Alice Jane Bellerd! It was all — all — I don't know. I said I loved her and wanted to marry her to get around somehow to make you smile. Yes, I said it because I planned to make you smile, that was the only reason. I'm never going to have a woman, I always knew for years I never would have. Will you please pass the potatoes, Aunt Rose?'

The front door splintered and fell. A heavy, softened rushing filled the hall. Men broke into the dining-room.

A hesitation.

The police inspector hastily removed his hat.

'Oh, I beg your pardon,' he apologized. 'I didn't mean to intrude upon your supper, I –'

The sudden halting of the police was such that their movement shook the room. The movement catapulted the bodies of Aunt Rose and Uncle Dimity straight away to the carpet, where they lay, their throats severed in a half-moon from ear to ear – which caused them, like the children seated at the table, to have what was the horrid illusion of a smile under their chins; ragged smiles that welcomed in the late arrivals and told them everything with a simple grimace . . .

The Handler

Mr Benedict came out of his little house. He stood on the porch, painfully shy of the sun and inferior to people. A little dog trotted by with clever eyes; so clever that Mr Benedict could not meet its gaze. A small child peered through the wrought-iron gate around the graveyard, near the church, and Mr Benedict winced at the pale penetrant curiosity of the child.

'You're the funeral man,' said the child.

Cringing within himself, Mr Benedict did not speak.

'You own the church?' asked the child, finally.

'Yes,' said Mr Benedict.

'And the funeral place?'

'Yes,' said Mr Benedict bewilderedly.

'And the yards and the stones and the graves?' wondered the child.

'Yes,' said Mr Benedict, with some show of pride. And it was true. An amazing thing it was. A stroke of business luck really, that had kept him busy and humming nights over long years. First he had landed the church and the churchyard, with a few green-mossed tombs, when the Baptist people moved uptown. Then he had built himself a fine little mortuary, in Gothic style, of course, and covered it with ivy, and then added a small house for himself, way in back. It was very convenient to die for Mr Benedict. He handled you in and out of buildings with a minimum of confusion and a maximum of synthetic benediction. No need of a funeral procession! declared his large advertisements in the morning paper. Out of the church and into the earth, slick as a whistle. Nothing but the finest preservatives used!

The child continued to stare at him and he felt like a candle blown out in the wind. He was so very inferior. Anything that lived or moved made him feel apologetic and melancholy. He was continually agreeing with people, never daring to argue or shout or say no. Whoever you might be, if Mr Benedict met you on the street he would look up your nostrils or perceive your ears or examine your hairline with his little shy, wild eyes and never look you straight in your eyes and he would hold your hand between his cold ones as if your hand was a precious gift as he said to you:

'You are definitely, irrevocably, believably correct.'

But, always, when you talked to him, you felt he never heard a word you said.

Now, he stood on his porch and said, 'You are a sweet little child,' to the little staring child, in fear that the child might not like him.

Mr Benedict walked down the steps and out the gate, without once looking at his little mortuary building. He saved that pleasure for later. It was very important that things took the right precedence. It wouldn't pay to think with joy of the bodies awaiting his talents in the mortuary building. No, it was better to follow his usual day-after-day routine. He would let the conflict begin.

He knew just where to go to get himself enraged. Half of the day he spent travelling from place to place in the little town, letting the superiority of the living neighbours overwhelm him, letting his own inferiority dissolve him, bathe him in perspiration, tie his heart and brain into trembling knots.

He spoke with Mr Rodgers, the druggist, idle, senseless morning talk. And he saved and put away all the little slurs and intonations and insults that Mr Rodgers sent his way. Mr Rodgers always had some terrible thing to say about a man in the funeral profession. 'Ha, ha,' laughed Mr Benedict at the latest joke upon himself, and he wanted to cry with miserable violence. 'There you are, you cold one,' said Mr Rodgers on this particular morning. 'Cold one,' said Mr Benedict. 'Ha, ha!'

Outside the drug-store, Mr Benedict met up with Mr Stuyvesant, the contractor. Mr Stuyvesant looked at his watch to estimate just how much time he dared waste on Benedict before trumping up some appointment. 'Oh, hello, Benedict,' shouted Stuyvesant. 'How's business? I bet you're going at it tooth and nail. Did you get it? I said, I bet you're going at it tooth and –' 'Yes, yes,' chuckled Mr Benedict vaguely. 'And how is your business, Mr Stuyvesant?' 'Say, how do your hands get so cold, Benny old man? That's a cold shake you got there. You just get done embalming a frigid woman? Hey, that's not bad. You heard what I said?' roared Mr Stuyvesant, pounding him on the back. 'Good, good!' cried Mr Benedict, with a fleshless smile. 'Good day.'

On it went, person after person. Mr Benedict, pummelled on from one to the next, was the lake into which all refuse was thrown. People began with little pebbles and then when Mr Benedict did not ripple or protest, they heaved a stone, a brick, a boulder. There was no bottom to Mr Benedict, no splash and no settling. The lake did not answer.

As the day passed he became more helpless and enraged with them, and he walked from building to building and had more little meetings and conversations and hated himself with a very real, masochistic pleasure. But the thing that kept him going most of all was the thought of the night pleasures to come. So he inflicted himself again and again with these stupid, pompous bullies and bowed to them and held his hands like little biscuits before his stomach, and asked for more than to be sneered at.

'There you are, meat-chopper,' said Mr Flinger, the delicatessen man. 'How are all your corned beeves and picked brains?'

Things worked to a crescendo of inferiority. With a final kettle-drumming of insult and terrible self-effacement, Mr Benedict, seeking wildly the correct time from his wrist watch, turned and ran back through the town. He was at his peak, he was all ready now, ready to work, ready to do what must be done, and enjoy himself. The awful part of the day was over, the good part was now to begin! He ran eagerly up the steps to his mortuary.

The room waited like a fall of snow. There were white hummocks and pale delineations of things recumbent under sheets in the dimness.

The door burst open.

Mr Benedict, framed in a flow of light, stood in the door, head back, one hand upraised in dramatic salute, the other hand upon the door-knob in unnatural rigidity.

He was the puppet-master come home.

He stood a long minute in the very centre of his theatre. In his head applause, perhaps, thundered. He did not move, but lowered his head in abject appreciation of this kind, kind applauding audience.

He carefully removed his coat, hung it up, got himself into a fresh white smock, buttoned the cuffs with professional crispness, then washed his hands together as he looked around at his very good friends.

It had been a fine week; there were any number of family relics lying under the sheets, and as Mr Benedict stood before them he felt himself grow and grow and tower and stretch over them.

'Like Alice!' he cried to himself in surprise. 'Taller, taller. Curiouser and curiouser!' He flexed his hands straight out and up.

He had never gotten over his initial incredulity when in the room with the dead. He was both delighted and bewildered to discover that here he was master of peoples, here he might do what he wished with men, and they must, by necessity, be polite and co-operative with him. They could not run away. And now, as on other days, he felt himself released and resilient, growing, growing like Alice. 'Oh, so tall, oh, so tall, so very tall . . . until my head . . . bumps . . . the ceiling.'

He walked about among the sheeted people. He felt the same as he did when coming from a picture show late at night, very strong, very alert, very certain of himself. He felt that everyone was watching him as he left a picture show, and that he was very handsome and very correct and brave and all the things that the picture hero was, his voice oh, so resonant, persuasive, and he had the right lilt to his left eyebrow and the right tap with his cane – and sometimes this movie-induced hypnosis lasted all the way home and persisted into sleep. Those were the only two times in his living he felt miraculous and fine, at the picture show, or here – in his own little theatre of the cold.

He walked along the sleeping rows, noting each name on its white card.

'Mrs Walters. Mr Smith. Miss Brown. Mr Andrews. Ah, good afternoon, one and all!'

'How are you today, Mrs Shellmund?' he wanted to know, lifting a sheet as if looking for a child under a bed. 'You're looking splendid, dear lady.'

Mrs Shellmund had never spoken to him in her life; she'd always gone by like a large white statue with roller skates hidden under her skirts, which gave her an elegant gliding, imperturbable rush.

'My dear Mrs Shellmund,' he said, pulling up a chair and regarding her through a magnifying-glass. 'Do you realize, my lady, that you have a sebaceous condition of the pores? You were quite waxen in life. Pore trouble. Oil and grease and pimples. A rich, rich diet, Mrs Shellmund, there was your trouble. Too many frosties and spongy cakes and cream candies. You always prided yourself on your brain, Mrs Shellmund, and thought I was like a dime under your toe, or a penny, really. But you kept that wonderful priceless brain of yours afloat in parfaits and fizzes and limeades and sodas and were so very superior to me that now, Mrs Shellmund, here is what shall happen . . .'

He did a neat operation on her. Cutting the scalp in a circle, he lifted it off, then lifted out the brain. Then he prepared a cake-confectioner's little sugar-bellows and squirted her empty head full of little whipped cream and crystal ribbons, stars and frollops, in pink, white and green, and on top he printed in a fine pink scroll SWEET DREAMS and put the skull back on and sewed it in place and hid the marks with wax and powder. 'So there,' he said, finished.

He walked on to the next table.

'Good afternoon, Mr Wren. Good afternoon. And how is the master of the racial hatreds today, Mr Wren? Pure, white, laundered Mr Wren. Clean as snow, white as linen. Mr Wren, you are. The man who hated Jews and negroes. Minorities, Mr Wren, minorities.' He pulled back the sheet. Mr Wren stared up with glassy cold eyes. 'Mr Wren, look upon a member of a minority. Myself. The minority of inferiors, those who speak not above a whisper, those afraid of talking aloud, those frightened little nonentities, mice. Do you know what I am going to do with you, Mr Wren? First, let us draw your blood from you, intolerant friend.' The blood was drawn off. 'Now – the injection of, you might say, embalming fluid.'

Mr Wren, snow-white, linen-pure, lay with the fluid going in him.

Mr Benedict laughed.

Mr Wren turned black; black as dirt, black as night.

The embalming fluid was – ink.

'And hello to *you*, Edmund Worth!'

What a handsome body Worth had. Powerful, with muscles pinned from huge bone to huge bone, and a chest like a boulder. Women had grown speechless when he walked by, men had stared with envy and hoped they might borrow that body some night and ride home in it to the wife and give her a nice surprise. But Worth's body had always been his own, and he had applied it to those tasks and pleasures which made him a conversational topic among all people who enjoyed sin.

'And now, here you are,' said Mr Benedict, looking down at the fine body with pleasure. For a moment he was lost in memory of his own body in his own past.

He had once tried strangling himself with one of those apparatuses you nail in a doorway and chuck under your jaw-bone and pull yourself up on, hoping to add an inch to his ridiculously short frame. To counteract his deadly pale skin he had lain in the sun, but he boiled and his skin fell off in pink leaflets, leaving only more pink, moist, sensitive skin. And what could he do about the eyes from which his mind peered, those close-set, glassy little eyes and the tiny wounded mouth? You can repaint houses, burn trash, move from the slum, shoot your mother, buy new clothes, get a car, make money, change all those outer environmentals for something new. But what's the brain to do when caught like cheese in the throat of a mouse? His own environment thus betrayed him; his own skin, body, colour, voice gave him no chance to extend out into that vast bright world where people tickled ladies' chins and kissed their mouths and shook hands with friends and traded aromatic cigars.

Thinking in this fashion, Mr Benedict stood over the magnificent body of Edmund Worth.

He severed Worth's head, put it in a coffin on a small satin pillow, facing up, then he placed one hundred and ninety pounds of bricks in the coffin and arranged some pillows inside a black coat and a white shirt and tie to look like the upper body, and covered the whole with a blanket of blue velvet, up to the chin. It was a fine illusion.

The body itself he placed in a refrigerating vault.

'When I die, I shall leave specific orders, Mr Worth, that my head be severed and buried, joined to your body. By that time I shall have acquired an assistant willing to perform such a rascally act, for money. If one cannot have a body worthy of love in life, one can at least gain such a body in death. Thank you.'

He slammed the lid on Edmund Worth.

Since it was a growing and popular habit in the town for people to be buried with the coffin lids closed over them during the service, this gave Mr Benedict great opportunities to vent his repressions on his hapless guests. Some he locked in their boxes upside down, some face down, or making obscene gestures. He had the most utterly wondrous fun with a group of old maiden ladies who were mashed in a car on their way to an afternoon tea. They were famous gossips, always with heads together over some choice bit. What the onlookers at the triple funeral did not know (all three casket lids were shut) was that, as in life, all three were crowded into one casket, heads together in eternal, cold, petrified gossip. The other two caskets were filled with pebbles and shells and ravels of gingham. It was a nice service. Everybody cried. 'Those three inseparables, at last separated,' everybody sobbed.

'Yes,' said Mr Benedict, having to hide his face in his grief.

Not lacking for a sense of justice, Mr Benedict buried one rich man stark naked. A poor man he buried wound in gold cloth, with five-dollar gold pieces for buttons and twenty-dollar coins on each eyelid. A lawyer he did not bury at all, but burnt him in the incinerator – his coffin contained nothing but a polecat, trapped in the woods one Sunday.

An old maid, at her service one afternoon, was the victim of a terrible device. Under the silken comforter, parts of an old man had been buried with her. There she lay, insulted by cold organs, being made cold love to by hidden hands, hidden and planted other things. The shock showed on her face, somewhat.

So Mr Benedict moved from body to body in his mortuary that afternoon, talking to all the sheeted figures, telling them his every secret. The final body for the day was the body of one Merriwell Blythe, an ancient man afflicted with spells and comas. Mr Blythe had been brought in for dead several times, but each time had revived in time to prevent premature burial.

Mr Benedict pulled back the sheet from Mr Blythe's face.

Mr Merriwell Blythe fluttered his eyes.

'Ah!' and Mr Benedict let fall the sheet.

'You!' screamed the voice under the sheet.

Mr Benedict fell against the slab, suddenly shaken and sick.

'Get me up from here!' cried the voice of Mr Merriwell Blythe.

'You're alive!' said Mr Benedict, jerking aside the sheet.

'Oh, the things I've heard, the things I've listened to the last hour!' wailed the old man on the slab, rolling his eyes about in his head in white orbits. 'Lying here, not able to move, and hearing you talk the things you talk! Oh, you dark, dark thing, you awful thing, you fiend, you monster, get me up from here. I'll tell the mayor and the council and everyone, oh, you dark, dark thing! You defiler and sadist, you perverted scoundrel, you terrible man, wait'll I tell, I tell on you!' shrieked the old man, frothing. 'Get me up from here!' 'No!' said Mr Benedict, falling to his knees. 'Oh, you terrible man!' sobbed Mr Merriwell Blythe. 'To think this has gone on in our town all these years and we never knew the things you did to people! Oh, you monstrous monster!' 'No,' whispered Mr Benedict, trying to get up, falling down, palsied and in terror. 'The things you *said*,' accused the old man in dry contempt. 'The things you do!' 'Sorry,' whispered Mr Benedict.

The old man tried to rise. 'Don't!' said Mr Benedict, and held on to him. 'Let go of me!' said the old man. 'No,' said Mr Benedict. He reached for a hypodermic and stabbed the old man in the arm with it. 'You!' cried the old man, wildly, to all the sheeted figures. 'Help me!' He squinted blindly at the window, at the churchyard below with the leaning stones. 'You, out there, too, under the stones, help! Listen!' The old man fell back, whistling and frothing. He knew he was dying. 'All, listen,' he babbled. 'He's done this to me, and you, and you, all of you, he's done too much, too long. Don't take it! Don't, don't let him do any more to anyone!' The old man licked away the stuff from his lips, growing weaker. 'Do something to him!'

Mr Benedict stood there, shocked, and said, 'They can't do anything to me. They can't. I say they can't.'

'Out of your graves!' wheezed the old man. 'Help me! Tonight, or tomorrow or soon, but jump up and fix him, oh, this horrible man!' And he wept many tears.

'How foolish,' said Mr Benedict numbly. 'You're dying and foolish.' Mr Benedict could not move his lips. His eyes were wide. 'Go on and die, now, quickly.'

'Everybody up!' shouted the old man. 'Everybody out! Help!'

'Please don't talk any more,' said Mr Benedict. 'I really don't like to listen.'

The room was suddenly very dark. It was night. It was getting late. The old man raved on and on, getting weaker. Finally, smiling, he said, 'They've taken a lot from you, horrible man. Tonight, they'll do something.'

The old man died.

People say there was an explosion that night in the graveyard. Or rather, a series of explosions, a smell of strange things, a movement, a violence, a raving.

There was much light and lightning, and a kind of rain, and the church bells hammered and slung about in the belfry, and stones toppled and things swore oaths, and things flew through the air, and there was a chasing and a screaming, and many shadows and all the lights in the mortuary blazing on, and things moving inside and outside in swift jerks and shamblings, windows broke, doors were torn from hinges, leaves from trees, iron gates clattered, and in the end there was a picture of Mr Benedict running about, running about, vanishing, the lights out, suddenly, and a tortured scream that could only be from Mr Benedict himself.

After that – nothing. Quiet.

The town people entered the mortuary the next morning. They searched the mortuary building and the church, and then they went out into the graveyard.

And they found nothing but blood, a vast quantity of blood, sprinkled and thrown and spread everywhere you could possibly look, as if the heavens had bled profusely in the night.

But not a sign of Mr Benedict.

'Where could he be?' everybody wondered.

'How should *we* know?' everybody replied, confounded.

And then they had the answer.

Walking through the graveyard they stood in deep tree shadows where the stones, row on row, were old and time-erased and leaning. No birds sang in the trees. The sunlight which finally managed to pierce the thick leaves, was like a light bulb illumination, weak, frail, unbelievable, theatrical, thin.

They stopped by one tombstone. 'Here, now!' they exclaimed.

Others paused and bent over the greyish, moss-flecked stone, and cried out.

Freshly scratched, as if by feebly, frantic, hasty fingers

(in fact, as if scratched by fingernails, the writing was that new) was the name: *MR BENEDICT*.

'Look over here!' someone else cried. Everybody turned. 'This one, this stone, and this one, and this one, too!' cried the villager, pointing to five other gravestones.

Everybody hurried around, looking and recoiling.

Upon each and every stone, scratched by fingernail scratchings, the same message appeared:

MR BENEDICT –

The town people were stunned.

'But that's impossible,' objected one of them, faintly. 'He *couldn't* be buried under *all* these gravestones!'

They stood there for one long moment. Instinctively they all looked at one another nervously in the silence and the tree darkness. They all waited for an answer. With fumbling, senseless lips, one of them replied, simply:

'*Couldn't* he?'

Let's Play 'Poison'

'We hate you!' cried the sixteen boys and girls rushing and crowding about Michael in the schoolroom. Michael screamed. Recess was over. Mr Howard, the teacher, was still absent from the filling room. 'We hate you!' and the sixteen boys and girls, bumping and clustering and breathing, raised a window. It was three flights down to the pavement. Michael flailed.

They took hold of Michael and pushed him out the window.

Mr Howard, their teacher, came into the room. 'Wait a minute!' he shouted.

Michael fell three flights. Michael died.

Nothing was done about it. The police shrugged eloquently. These children were all eight or nine, they didn't understand what they were doing. So.

Mr Howard's breakdown occurred the next day. He refused, ever again, to teach! 'But, why?' asked his friends. Mr Howard gave no answer. He remained silent and a terrible light filled his eyes, and later he remarked that if he told them the truth they would think him quite insane.

Mr Howard left Madison City. He went to live in a small nearby town, Green Bay, for seven years, on an income managed from writing stories and poetry.

He never married. The few women he approached always desired – children.

In the autumn of his seventh year of self-enforced retirement, a good friend of Mr Howard's, a teacher, fell ill. For lack of a proper substitute, Mr Howard was summoned and convinced that it was his duty to take over

the class. Because he realized the appointment could last no
longer than a few weeks, Mr Howard agreed, unhappily.

'Sometimes,' announced Mr Howard, slowly pacing the
aisles of the schoolroom on that Monday morning in
September, 'sometimes, I actually believe that children
are invaders from another dimension.'

He stopped, and his shiny dark eyes snapped from face
to face of his small audience. He held one hand behind him,
clenched. The other hand, like a pale animal, climbed his
lapel as he talked and later climbed back down to toy with
his ribboned glasses.

'Sometimes,' he continued, looking at William Arnold
and Russell Newell, and Donald Bowers and Charlie
Hencoop, 'sometimes I believe children are little monsters
thrust out of hell, because the devil could no longer cope
with them. And I certainly believe that everything should
be done to reform their uncivil little minds.'

Most of his words ran unfamiliarly into the washed and
unwashed ears of Arnold, Newell, Bowers and Company.
But the tone inspired one to dread. The little girls lay
back in their seats, against their pigtails, lest he yank them
like bell-ropes, to summon the dark angels. All stared at
Mr Howard, as if hypnotized.

'You are another race entirely, your motives, your
beliefs, your disobediences,' said Mr Howard. 'You are
not human. You are – children. Therefore, until such time
as you are adults, you have no right to demand privileges
or question your elders, who know better.'

He paused, and put his elegant rump upon the chair
behind the neat, dustless desk.

'Living in your world of fantasy,' he said, scowling darkly.
'Well, there'll be no fantasy here. You'll soon discover that
a ruler on your hand is no dream, no faerie frill, no Peter
Pan excitement.' He snorted. 'Have I frightened you? I
have. Good! Well and good. You deserve to be. I want you
to know where we stand. I'm not afraid of you, remember

that. I'm not afraid of you.' His hand trembled and he drew back in his chair as all their eyes stared at him. 'Here!' he flung a glance clear across the room. 'What're you whispering about, back there? Some necromancy or other?'

A little girl raised her hand. 'What's necromancy?'

'We'll discuss that when our two young friends, Mr Arnold and Mr Bowers, explain their whispers. Well, young men?'

Donald Bowers arose. 'We don't like you. That's all we said.' He sat down again.

Mr Howard raised his brows. 'I like frankness, truth. Thank you for your honesty. But, simultaneously, I do not tolerate flippant rebellion. You'll stay an hour after school tonight and wash the boards.'

After school, walking home, with autumn leaves falling both before and after his passing, Mr Howard caught up with four of his students. He rapped his cane sharply on the pavement.

'Here, what are you children doing?'

The two startled boys and girls jerked as if struck upon their shoulders by his cane. 'Oh,' they all said.

'Well,' demanded the man. 'Explain. What were you doing here when I came up?'

William Arnold said, 'Playing poison.'

'Poison!' Their teacher's face twisted. He was carefully sarcastic. 'Poison, poison, playing poison. Well. And how does one play poison?'

Reluctantly, William Arnold ran off.

'Come back here!' shouted Mr Howard.

'I'm only showing you,' said the boy, hopping over a cement block of the pavement, 'how we play poison. Whenever we come to a dead man we jump over him.'

'One does, does one?' said Mr Howard.

'If you jump on a dead man's grave, then you're poisoned and fall down and die,' explained Isabel Skelton, much too brightly.

'Dead men, graves, poisoned,' Mr Howard said, mockingly. 'Where do you get this dead man idea?'

'See?' said Clara Parris, pointing with her arithmetic. 'On this square, the name of the two dead men.'

'Ridiculous,' retorted Mr Howard, squinting down. 'Those are simply the names of the contractors who mixed and laid the cement pavement.'

Isabel and Clara both gasped wildly and turned accusing eyes to the two boys. 'You said they were gravestones!' they cried, almost together.

William Arnold looked at his feet. 'Yeah. They are. Well, almost. Anyway.' He looked up. 'It's late. I gotta go home. So long.'

Clara Parris looked at the two little names cut into the pavement. 'Mr Kelly and Mr Terrill,' she read the names. 'Then these aren't graves? Mr Kelly and Mr Terrill aren't buried here? See, Isabel, that's what I told you, a dozen times I did.'

'You did not,' sulked Isabel.

'Deliberate lies.' Mr Howard tapped his cane in an impatient code. 'Falsification of the highest calibre. Good God, Mr Arnold, Mr Bowers, there'll be no more of this, do you understand?'

'Yes, sir,' mumbled the boys.

'Speak up!'

'Yes, sir,' they replied, again.

Mr Howard swung off swiftly down the street. William Arnold waited until he was out of sight before he said, 'I hope a bird drops something right smack on his nose –'

'Come on, Clara, let's play poison,' said Isabel, hopefully.

Clara pouted. 'It's been spoiled. I'm going home.'

'I'm poisoned!' cried Donald Bowers, falling to the earth and frothing merrily. 'Look, I'm poisoned! Gahhh!'

'Oh,' cried Clara, angrily, and ran away.

*   *   *

Saturday morning Mr Howard glanced out of his front window and swore when he saw Isabel Skelton making chalk marks on his pavement and then hopping about, making a monotonous singsong with her voice.

'Stop that!'

Rushing out, he almost flung her to the pavement in his emotion. He grabbed her and shook her violently and let her go and stood over her and the chalk marks.

'I was only playing hopscotch,' she sobbed, hands over her eyes.

'I don't care, you can't play it here,' he declared. Bending, he erased the chalk marks with his handkerchief, muttering, 'Young witch. Pentagrams. Rhymes and incantations, and all looking perfectly innocent, God, how innocent. You little *fiend*!' he made as if to strike her, but stopped. Isabel ran off, wailing. 'Go ahead, you little fool!' he screamed, furiously. 'Run off and tell your little cohorts that you've failed. They'll have to try some other way! They won't get around me, they won't, oh, no!'

He stalked back into his house and poured himself a stiff drink of brandy and drank it down. The rest of the day he heard the children playing kick-the-can, hide-and-seek, Over-Annie-Over, jacks, tops, mibs, and the sound of the little monsters in every shrub and shadow would not let him rest. 'Another week of this,' he thought, 'and I'll be stark staring.' He flung his hand to his aching head. 'God in heaven, why weren't we all born adults?'

Another week, then. And the hatred growing between him and the children. The hate and the fear growing apace. The nervousness, the sudden tantrums over nothing, and then – the silent waiting, the way the children climbed the trees and looked at him as they swiped late apples, the melancholy smell of autumn settling in around the town, the days growing short, the night coming too soon.

'But they won't touch me, they won't *dare* touch me,' thought Mr Howard, sucking down one glass of brandy after another. 'It's all very silly anyhow, and there's nothing to it. I'll soon be away from here, and – them. I'll soon –'

There was a white skull at the window.

It was eight o'clock of a Thursday evening. It had been a long week, with the angry flares and the accusations. He had had to continually chase the children away from the water-main excavation in front of his house. Children loved excavations, hiding-places, pipes and conduits and trenches, and they were ever ascramble over and on and down in and up out of the holes where the new pipes were being laid. It was all finished, thank the Lord, and tomorrow the workmen would shovel in the earth and tamp it down and put in a new cement pavement, and that would eliminate the children. But, right now –

There was a white skull at the window!

There could be no doubt that a boy's hand held the skull against the glass, tapping and moving it. There was a childish tittering from outside.

Mr Howard burst from the house. 'Hey, you!' He exploded into the midst of the three running boys. He leaped after them, shouting and yelling. The street was dark, but he saw the figures dart beyond and below him. He saw them sort of bound and could not remember the reason for this, until too late.

The earth opened under him. He fell and lay in a pit, his head taking a terrific blow from a laid water-pipe, and as he lost consciousness he had an impression as of an avalanche, set off by his fall, cascading down cool moist pellets of dirt upon his pants, his shoes, upon his coat, upon his spine, upon the back of his neck, his head, filling his mouth, his ears, his eyes, his nostrils . . .

The neighbour lady with the eggs wrapped in a napkin, knocked on Mr Howard's door the next day for five minutes. When she opened the door, finally, and walked in, she found nothing but specules of rug-dust floating in the sunny air, the big halls were empty, the cellar smelled of coal and clinkers, and the attic had nothing in it but a rat, a spider, and a faded letter. 'Funniest thing,' she said many times in the following years, 'whatever happened to Mr Howard.'

And adults, being what they are, never observant, paid no attention to the children playing 'Poison' on Oak Bay Street, in all the following autumns. Even when the children leaped over one particular square of cement, twisted about and glanced at the marks on it which read:

'M. HOWARD – R.I.P.'

'Who's Mr Howard, Billy?'

'Aw, I guess he's the guy who laid the cement.'

'What does R.I.P. mean?'

'Aw, who knows? You're poison! You stepped on it!'

'Get along, get along, children; don't stand in Mother's path! Get along now!'

The Night

You are a child in a small town. You are, to be exact, eight years old, and it is growing late at night. Late, for you, accustomed to bedding in at nine or nine-thirty; once in a while perhaps begging Mom or Dad to let you stay up later to hear Sam and Henry on that strange radio that is popular in this year of 1927. But most of the time you are in bed and snug at this time of night.

It is a warm summer evening. You live in a small house on a small street in the outer part of town where there are few street lights. There is only one store open, about a block away; Mrs Singer's. In the hot evening Mother has been ironing the Monday wash and you have been intermittently begging for ice-cream and staring into the dark.

You and your mother are all alone at home in the warm darkness of summer. Finally, just before it is time for Mrs Singer to close her store, Mother relents and tells you:

'Run get a pint of ice-cream and be sure she packs it tight.'

You ask if you can get a scoop of chocolate ice-cream on top, because you don't like vanilla, and Mother agrees. You clutch the money and run barefooted over the warm evening cement pavement, under the apple trees and oak trees, towards the store. The town is so quiet and far off, you can only hear the crickets sounding in the spaces beyond the hot indigo trees that hold back the stars.

Your bare feet slap the pavement, you cross the street and find Mrs Singer moving ponderously about her store, singing Yiddish melodies.

'Pint ice-cream?' she says. 'Chocolate on top? Yes!'

You watch her fumble the metal top off the ice-cream freezer and manipulate the scoop, packing the cardboard pint chock full with 'chocolate on top, yes!' You give the money, receive the chill, icy pack, and rubbing it across your brow and cheek, laughing, you thump barefootedly homeward. Behind you, the lights of the lonely little store blink out and there is only a street light shimmering on the corner, and the whole city seems to be going to sleep . . .

Opening the screen door you find Mom still ironing. She looks hot and irritated, but she smiles just the same.

'When will Dad be home from lodge-meeting?' you ask.

'About eleven-thirty or twelve,' Mother replies. She takes the ice-cream to the kitchen, divides it. Giving you your special portion of chocolate, she dishes out some for herself and the rest is put away, 'For Skipper and your father when they come.'

Skipper is your brother. He is your older brother. He's twelve and healthy, red-faced, hawk-nosed, tawny-haired, broad-shouldered for his years, and always running. He is allowed to stay up later than you. Not much later, but enough to make him feel it is worth while having been born first. He is over on the other side of town this evening to a game of kick-the-can and will be home soon. He and the kids have been yelling, kicking, running for hours, having fun. Soon he will come clomping in, smelling of sweat and green grass on his knees where he fell, and smelling very much in all ways like Skipper; which is natural.

You sit enjoying the ice-cream. You are at the core of the deep quiet summer night. Your mother and yourself and the night all around this small house on this small street. You lick each spoon of ice-cream thoroughly before digging for another, and Mom puts her ironing-board away and the hot iron in its case, and she sits in the armchair by the phonograph, eating her dessert and saying, 'My lands, it was a hot day today. It's still hot. Earth soaks up all the heat and lets it out at night. It'll be soggy sleeping.'

You both sit there listening to the summer silence. The dark is pressed down by every window and door, there is no sound because the radio needs a new battery, and you have played all the Knickerbocker Quartet records and Al Jolson and Two Black Crows records to exhaustion; so you just sit on the hardwood floor by the door and look out into the dark dark dark, pressing your nose against the screen until the flesh of its tip is moulded into small dark squares.

'I wonder where your brother is?' Mother says after a while. Her spoon scrapes on the dish. 'He should be home by now. It's almost nine-thirty.'

'He'll be here,' you say, knowing very well that he will be.

You follow Mom out to wash the dishes. Each sound, each rattle of spoon or dish is amplified in the baked evening. Silently, you go to the living-room, remove the couch cushions and, together, yank it open and extend it down into the double bed that it secretly is. Mother makes the bed, punching pillows neatly to flump them up for your head. Then, as you are unbuttoning your shirt, she says:

'Wait a while, Doug.'

'Why?'

'Because. I say so.'

'You look funny, Mom.'

Mom sits down a moment, then stands up, goes to the door, and calls. You listen to her calling and calling Skipper, Skipper, Skiiiiiiiperrrrrrr over and over. Her calling goes out into the summer-warm dark and never comes back. The echoes pay no attention.

Skipper.

Skipper!

And as you sit on the floor a coldness that is not ice-cream and not winter, and not part of summer's heat, goes through you. You notice Mom's eyes sliding, blinking; the way she stands undecided and is nervous. All of these things.

She opens the screen door. Stepping out into the night she walks down the steps and down the front sidewalk under the lilac bush. You listen to her moving feet.

She calls again. Silence.

She calls twice more. You sit in the room. Any moment now Skipper will reply, from down the long, long narrow street:

'All right, Mom! All right, Mother! Hey!'

But he doesn't answer. And for two minutes you sit looking at the made-up bed, the silent radio, the silent phonograph, at the chandelier with its crystal bobbins gleaming quietly, at the rug with the scarlet and purple curlicues on it. You stub your toe on the bed purposely to see if it hurts. It does.

Whining, the screen door opens, and Mother says:

'Come on, Shorts. We'll take a walk.'

'Where to?'

'Just down the block. Come on. Better put your shoes on, though. You'll catch cold.'

'No, I won't. I'll be all right.'

You take her hand. Together you walk down St James Street. You smell lilacs in blossom; fallen apples lying crushed and odorous in the deep grass. Underfoot, the concrete is still warm, and the crickets are sounding louder against the darkening dark. You reach a corner, turn, and walk towards the ravine.

Off somewhere, a car goes by, flashing its lights in the distance. There is such a complete lack of life, light and activity. Here and there, back off from where you are walking towards the ravine, you see faint squares of light where people are still up. But most of the houses, darkened, are sleeping already, and there are a few lightless places where the occupants of a dwelling sit talking low dark talk on their front porches. You hear a porch swing squeaking as you walk near.

'I wish your father was home,' says Mother. Her large hand tightens around your small one. 'Just wait'll I get that boy. I'll spank him within an inch of his life.'

A razor strop hangs in the kitchen for this. You think of it, remember when Dad has doubled and flourished it with muscled control over your frantic limbs. You doubt Mother will carry out her promise.

Now you have walked another block and are standing by the holy black silhouette of the German Baptist Church at the corner of Chapel Street and Glen Rock. In back of the church a hundred yards away, the ravine begins. You can smell it. It has a dark sewer, rotten foliage, thick green odour. It is a wide ravine that cuts and twists across the town, a jungle by day, a place to let alone at night, Mother has often declared.

You should feel encouraged by the nearness of the German Baptist Church, but you are not – because the building is not illumined, is cold and useless as a pile of ruins on the ravine edge.

You are only eight years old, you know little of death, fear, or dread. Death is the waxen effigy in the coffin when you were six and Grandfather passed away – looking like a great fallen vulture in his casket, silent, withdrawn, no more to tell you how to be a good boy, no more to comment succinctly on politics. Death is your little sister one morning when you awaken at the age of seven, look into her crib and see her staring up at you with a blind blue, fixed and frozen stare until the men came with a small wicker basket to take her away. Death is when you stand by her high-chair four weeks later and suddenly realize she'll never be in it again, laughing and crying and making you jealous of her because she was born. That is death.

But this is more than death. This summer night wading deep in time and stars and warm eternity. It is an essence of all the things you will ever feel or see or hear in your life again, being brought steadily home to you all at once.

Leaving the pavement, you walk along a trodden, pebbled, weed-fringed path to the ravine's edge. Crickets, in loud full drumming chorus now, are shouting to quiver the dead. You follow obediently behind brave, fine, tall Mother who is defender of all the universe. You feel braveness because she goes before, and you hang back a trifle for a moment, and then hurry on, too. Together, then, you approach, reach and pause at the very edge of civilization.

The ravine.

Here and now, down there in that pit of jungled blackness is suddenly all the evil you will ever know. Evil you will never understand. All of the nameless things are there. Later, when you have grown you'll be given names to label them with. Meaningless syllables to describe the waiting nothingness. Down there in the huddled shadow, among thick trees and trailed vines, lives the odour of decay. Here, at this spot, civilization ceases, reason ends, and a universal evil takes over.

You realize you are alone. You and your mother. Her hand trembles.

Her hand *trembles*.

Your belief in your private world is shattered. You feel Mother tremble. Why? Is she, too, doubtful? But she is bigger, stronger, more intelligent than yourself, isn't she? Does she, too, feel that intangible menace, that groping out of darkness, that crouching malignancy down below? Is there, then, no strength in growing up? no solace in being an adult? no sanctuary in life? no flesh citadel strong enough to withstand the scrabbling assault of midnights? Doubts flush you. Ice-cream lives again in your throat, stomach, spine and limbs; you are instantly cold as a wind out of December-gone.

You realize that all men are like this. That each person is

to himself one alone. One oneness, a unit in a society, but always afraid. Like here, standing. If you should scream now, if you should holler for help, would it matter?

You are so close to the ravine now that in the instant of your scream, in the interval between someone hearing it and running to find you, much could happen.

Blackness could come swiftly, swallowing; and in one titanically freezing moment all would be concluded. Long before dawn, long before police with flashlights might probe the disturbed pathway, long before men with trembling brains could rustle down the pebbles to your help. Even if they were within five hundred yards of you now, and help *certainly* is, in three seconds a dark tide could rise to take all eight years of life away from you and –

The essential impact of life's loneliness crushes your beginning-to-tremble body. Mother is alone, too. She cannot look to the sanctity of marriage, the protection of her family's love, she cannot look to the United States Constitution or the City Police, she cannot look anywhere, in this very instant, save into her heart, and there she'll find nothing but uncontrollable repugnance and a will to fear. In this instant it is an individual problem seeking an individual solution. You must accept being alone and work on from there.

You swallow hard, cling to her. Oh, Lord, don't let her die, please, you think. Don't do anything to us. Father will be coming home from lodge-meeting in an hour and if the house is empty . . . ?

Mother advances down the path into the primeval jungle. Your voice trembles. 'Mom. Skip's all right. Skip's all right. He's all right. Skip's all right.'

Mother's voice is strained high. 'He always comes through here. I tell him not to, but those darned kids, they come through here anyway. Some night he'll come through and never come out again –'

Never come out again. That could mean anything.

Tramps. Criminals. Darkness. Accident. Most of all –
death.

Alone in the universe.

There are a million small towns like this all over the
world. Each as dark, as lonely, each as removed, as full
of shuddering and wonder. The reedy playing of minor-key
violins is the small towns' music, with no lights but many
shadows. Oh the vast swelling loneliness of them. The
secret damp ravines of them. Life is a horror lived in
them at night, when at all sides sanity, marriage, children,
happiness, is threatened by an ogre called Death.

Mother raises her voice into the dark.

'Skip! Skipper!' she calls. 'Skip! Skipper!'

Suddenly, both of you realize there is something wrong.
Something very wrong. You listen intently and realize what
it is. The crickets have stopped chirping.

Silence is complete.

Never in your life a silence like this one. One so utterly
complete. Why should the crickets cease? Why? What
reason? They have never stopped ever before. Not ever.

Unless. Unless –

Something is going to happen.

It is as if the whole ravine is tensing, bunching together
its black fibres, drawing in power from all about sleeping
countrysides, for miles and miles. From dew-sodden forest
and dells and rolling hills where dogs tilt heads to moons,
from all around the great silence is sucked into one centre,
and you at the core of it. In ten seconds now, something
will happen, something will happen. The crickets keep their
truce, the stars are so low you can almost brush the tinsel.
There are swarms of them, hot and sharp.

Growing, growing, the silence. Growing, growing the
tenseness. Oh it's so dark, so far away from everything.
Oh God!

And then, way way off across the ravine:

'Okay Mom! Coming, Mother!'

And again:

'Hi, Mom! Coming, Mom!'

And then the quick scuttering of tennis shoes padding down through the pit of the ravine as three kids come dashing, giggling. Your brother Skipper, Chuck Redman and Augie Bartz. Running, giggling.

The stars suck up like the stung antennae of ten million snails.

The crickets sing!

The darkness pulls back, startled, shocked, angry. Pulls back, losing its appetite at being so rudely interrupted as it prepared to feed. As the dark retreats like a wave on a shore, three kids pile out of it, laughing.

'Hi, Mom! Hi, Shorts! Hey!'

It smells like Skipper all right. Sweat and grass and his oiled leather baseball glove.

'Young man, you're going to get a licking,' declares Mother. She puts away her fear instantly. You know she will never tell anybody of it, ever. It will be in her heart though, for all time, as it is in your heart, for all time.

You walk home to bed in the late summer night. You are glad Skipper is alive. Very glad. For a moment there you thought —

Far off in the dim moonlit country, over a viaduct and down a valley, a train goes rushing along and it whistles like a lost metal thing, nameless and running. You go to bed, shivering, beside your brother, listening to that train whistle, and thinking of a cousin who lived way out in the country where that train is now; a cousin who died of pneumonia late at night years and years ago . . . You smell the sweat of Skip beside you. It is magic. You stop trembling. You hear footsteps outside the house on the sidewalk, as Mother is turning out the lights. A man clears his throat in a way you recognize.

Mom says, 'That's your father.'

It is.

The Dead Man

'That's the man, right over there,' said Mrs Ribmoll, nodding across the street. 'See that man perched on the tar barrel afront Mr Jenkens's store? Well, that's him. They call him Odd Martin.'

'The one that says he's dead?' cried Arthur.

Mrs Ribmoll nodded. 'Crazy as a weasel down a chimney. Carries on firm about how he's been dead since the Flood and nobody appreciates it.'

'I see him sitting there every day,' cried Arthur.

'Oh, yes, he sits there, he does. Sits there and stares at nothing. I say it's a crying shame they don't throw him in jail!'

Arthur made a face at the man. 'Yah!'

'Never mind, he won't notice you. Most uncivil man I ever seen. Nothing pleases him.' She yanked Arthur's arm. 'Come on, sonny, we got shopping to do.'

They walked on up the street past the barber shop. In the window, after they'd gone by, stood Mr Simpson, snipping his blue shears and chewing his tasteless gum. He squinted thoughtfully out through the fly-specked glass, looking at the man sitting over there on the tar barrel. 'I figure the best thing could happen to Odd Martin would be to get married,' he figured. His eyes glinted slyly. Over his shoulder he looked at his manicurist, Miss Weldon, who was busy burnishing the scraggly fingernails of a farmer named Gilpatrick. Miss Weldon, at this suggestion, did not look up. She had heard it often. They were always ragging her about Odd Martin.

Mr Simpson walked back and started work on Gilpatrick's dusty hair again. Gilpatrick laughed softly. 'What woman would marry Odd? Sometimes I almost believe he *is* dead. He's got an awful odour to him.'

Miss Weldon looked up at Mr Gilpatrick's face and carefully cut his finger with one of her little scalpels. 'God darn it!' He jumped. 'Watch what you're doin', woman!'

Miss Weldon looked at him with calm little blue eyes in a small white face. Her hair was mouse-brown; she wore no make-up and talked to no one most of the time.

Mr Simpson cackled and snicked his blue steel shears. 'Hope, hope, hope!' he laughed like that. 'Miss Weldon, she knows what she's doin', Gilpatrick. Just you be careful, Miss Weldon, he give a bottle of eau de cologne to Odd Martin last Christmas. It helped cover up his smell.'

Miss Weldon laid down her instruments.

'Sorry, Miss Weldon,' apologized Mr Simpson. 'I won't say no more.'

Reluctantly, she took up her instruments again.

'Hey!' cried one of the four other men waiting in the shop. 'There he goes *again*!' Mr Simpson whirled, almost taking Gilpatrick's pink ear with him in his shears. 'Come look, boys!'

Across the street the sheriff stepped out of his office door just then and he saw it happen, too. He saw what Odd Martin was doing.

Everybody came running from all the little stores.

The sheriff walked over and looked down into the gutter.

'Come on, now, Odd Martin, come on now,' he shouted. He poked down into the gutter with his shiny black boot-tip. 'Come on, get up! You're not dead. You're good as me. You'll catch your death of cold there with all them gum wrappers and cigar butts. Come on, get up!'

Mr Simpson arrived on the scene and looked at Odd Martin lying there. 'He looks like a bottle a milk.'

'He's takin' up valuable parkin' space for cars, this bein'

Friday mornin',' whined the sheriff. 'And lots of people needin' the area. Here now, *Odd*! Hmm. Well . . . give me a hand here, boys.'

They lifted the body up on to the sidewalk.

'Let him stay here,' declared the sheriff, jostling around in his boots. 'Just let him stay till he gets tired of layin'. He's done this a million times before. Likes the publicity. Vamoose, you kids!'

He sent a bunch of children skipping ahead of his cheek of tobacco.

Back in the barber shop, Simpson looked around. 'Where's Miss Weldon? Unh.' He looked through the window. 'There she is, brushing him off again, while he lies there. Fixing his coat, buttoning it up. Here she comes back. Don't nobody fun with her, she resents it.'

The barber clock said twelve and then one and then two and then three. Mr Simpson kept track of it. 'I make you a bet that Odd Martin lies over there till four o'clock,' he said.

Someone else said, 'I'll bet he's there until four-thirty.'

'Last time' – a snickering of the shears – 'he was there five hours. Nice warm day today. He may snooze there until six. I'll say six. Let's see your money, gents!'

The money was put on the shelf by the hair-ointments.

One of the younger men shaved a stick with his penknife. 'It's sorta funny how we joke about Odd. Sometimes I wonder if we ain't really just scared of him, inside us. I mean, we won't let ourselves believe he's really dead. We don't dare believe it. We'd never get over it if we knew. So we make him a kinda joke. We let him lay around. He don't hurt nobody. He's just there. But I notice old Sawbones Hudson's never really touched Odd's heart with his stethoscope. Scared of what he'd find, I bet.'

'Scared of what he'd find!' Laughter. Simpson laughed and snished his shears. Two men with crusty beards laughed, a little too loud. The laughter didn't last long.

'Great one for jokin', you are!' they all said, slapping their gaunt knees.

Miss Weldon, she went on manicuring her clients.

'He's gettin' up!'

There was a general half-rising of all the bodies in the shop and a lot of neck twisting to watch Odd Martin gain his feet. 'He's up on one knee, now up on the other, now someone's givin' him a hand.'

'It's Miss Weldon. She sure got over there in a rush!'

'What time is it?'

'Four-fifteen! You lose, Simp! Pay us!'

The bet was settled.

'That Miss Weldon's a queer beetle herself. Takin' after a man like Odd.'

Simpson clicked his scissors. 'Being an orphan, she's got quiet ways. She likes men who don't say much. Odd, he don't say hardly anything. Just the opposite of us crude, crude men, eh, fellows? We talk too much. Miss Weldon don't like our way of speakin'.'

'There they go. The two of 'em. Miss Weldon and Odd Martin.'

'Say, take a little more off around my ears, will you, Simp?'

Skipping down the street, bouncing a red rubber ball, came little Radney Bellows, his blond hair flopping in a yellow fringe over his blue eyes. He bounced the ball abstractedly, tongue between lips, and the ball fell under Odd Martin's feet where he sat once more on the tar barrel. Inside the grocery, Miss Weldon was doing her supper shopping, putting soup cans and vegetable cans into a basket.

'Can I have my ball?' asked little Radney Bellows upwards at the six feet two inches of Odd Martin. No one was within hearing distance.

'Can you have your ball?' said Odd Martin haltingly. He turned it over inside his head, it appeared. His level, grey eyes shaped up Radney like one would shape up a little ball of clay. 'You can have your ball, yes; take it.'

Radney bent slowly and took hold of the bright red rubber globe and arose slowly, a secretive look in his eyes.

'I know something.'

Odd Martin looked down. 'You know something?'

Radney leaned forward. 'You're *dead*.'

Odd Martin sat there.

'You're really dead,' whispered little Radney Bellows. 'But I'm the only one who really knows. I believe you, Mr Odd. I tried it once myself. Dying, I mean. It's hard. It's work. I laid on the floor for an hour. But my stomach itched, so I scratched it, and the blood got up in my head and made me dizzy. Then – I quit. Why?' He looked at his shoes. ''Cause I had to go to the bathroom.'

A slow, understanding smile formed in the soft pallid flesh of Odd Martin's long, bony face. 'It *is* work. It isn't easy.'

'Sometimes, I think about you,' said Radney. 'I see you walk by my house. Nights. Sometimes two in the morning. I wake up. I know you're out walking around. I know I should look out, and I do, and, gee, there you are, walking and walking. Not going hardly any place.'

'There's no place to go.' Odd sat with his large, square, calloused hands on his knees. 'I try thinking of some – place to – go –' He slowed, like a horse to a bit-pull '– but it's hard to think. I try and – try. Sometimes I almost know what to do, where to go. Then, I forget. Once I had an idea to go to a doctor and have him declare me dead, but, somehow –' his voice was slow and husky and low '– I never got there.'

Radney looked straight at him. 'If you want, I'll take you.'

Odd Martin glanced leisurely at the setting sun. 'No. I'm weary, tired, but I'll – wait. Now I've gone this far,

I'm curious to see what happens next. After the flood that washed away my farm and all my stock and put me under water, like a chicken in a bucket, I filled up like you'd fill a thermos with water, and I came walking out of the flood, anyhow. But I knew I was dead. Late of nights I lay listening in my room, but there's no heartbeat in my ears or in my chest or in my wrists, though I lie still as a cold cricket. Nothing inside me but a darkness and a relaxation and an understanding. There must be a reason for me still walking, though. Maybe it was because I was still young when I died. Only twenty-eight, and not married yet. I always wanted to marry, never got around to it. Here I am, doing odd jobs around town, saving my money, 'cause I never eat, *heck*, I *can't* eat, and sometimes getting so discouraged and downright bewildered that I lie in the gutter and hope they'll take me and poke me in a pine box and lay me away for ripening. Yet, at the same time – I don't want that. I want a little more. I realize it whenever Miss Weldon walks by and I see the wind playing her hair like a little brown feather –' He sighed away into a pause.

Radney Bellows waited a minute, then cleared his throat and darted away, bouncing his ball. 'See you later!'

Odd stared at the spot where Radney had been. Five minutes later he blinked. 'Eh? Somebody here? Somebody speak?'

Miss Weldon came from the grocery with a basket of food.

'Like to walk me home, Odd?'

They walked along in a comfortable silence, she careful not to walk too fast, because he set his feet down carefully. The wind rustled in the cedars and in the elms and the maples all along the way. Several times his lips parted and he glanced aside at her, and then he shut his mouth tight and squinted ahead, as if looking at something a million miles off.

Finally, he said, 'Miss Weldon?'

'Yes, Odd?'

'I been saving and saving my money. I've got quite a handsome sum. I don't spend much for anything, and – you'd be surprised,' he said, sincerely. 'I got about a thousand dollars. Maybe more. Sometimes I count it and get tired and I can't count no more. And –' He seemed baffled and a little angry with her, suddenly. '*Why* do you like me, Miss Weldon?' he demanded.

She looked a little surprised, then smiled up at him. It was almost a child look of liking she gave him. 'Because. You're quiet. Because. You're not loud and mean. Like the men at the barber's. Because. I'm lonely, and you've been kind. Because you're the first one that ever looked at me. The others don't even see me, not once. They say I can't think. They say I'm senseless because I didn't finish sixth grade. But I'm so lonely, Odd, and talking to you means so much.'

He held her small white hand, tight.

She moistened her lips. 'I wish we could do something about the way people talk about you. I don't want to sound mean, but if you'd only stop telling them you're dead, Odd.'

He stopped walking. 'Then you don't believe me, either,' he said, remotely.

'You're "dead" for want of a good woman's cooking, for loving, for living decent, Odd. That's what you mean by "dead"; nothing else!'

His grey eyes were deep and lost. 'Is that what I mean?' He saw her eager, shiny face. 'Yes, that's what I mean. You guessed it right. That's what I mean.'

Their footsteps went along together, drifting in the wind, like leaves floating, and the night got darker and softer and the stars came out.

Two boys and two girls stood under a street lamp about nine o'clock that evening. Far away down the street someone walked along slowly, quietly, alone.

'There he is,' said one of the boys. '*You* ask him, Tom.'

Tom scowled uneasily. The girls laughed at him. Tom said, 'Okay, but you come along.'

Odd Martin walked along, pausing now and then to examine a fallen leaf with the tip of his shoe, turning and lifting it.

'Mr Odd? Hey there, Mr Odd!'

'Eh? Oh, hello.'

'Mr Odd, we –' Tom swallowed and looked around for assistance. 'That is – we want you to – well – we want you to come to our party!'

A minute later, after looking at Tom's clean, soap-smelling face and seeing the pretty blue jacket his sixteen-year-old girl friend wore, Odd answered. 'Thank you. But I don't know. I might forget to come.'

'No, you wouldn't. You'd remember, because this is Hallowe'en!'

Tom's girl pulled his arm. 'Let's go, Tom. Let's not have him. Let's not. Please. He won't do, Tom.'

'Why won't he do?'

'He's – he's not scary enough.'

Tom shook her off. 'Let *me* handle this.'

The girl pleaded. 'Please, no. He's just a dirty old man. Bill can put candle-tallow on his fingers and those horrid porcelain teeth in his mouth and the green chalk marks under his eyes and scare the ducks out of us. We don't need *him*!' And she perked her rebellious head at Odd.

Odd Martin stood watching the leaves under his shoe-tips. He heard the stars sitting in the sky for ten minutes before he knew the four young folks were gone. A round dry laugh came in his mouth like a pebble. Children.

Hallowe'en. Not scary enough. Bill'd do better. Candle-tallow and green chalk. Just an old man. He tasted the laughter, found it both strange and bitter.

Morning again. Radney Bellows flung his ball against the store front, caught it, flung it again. Someone hummed behind him. He turned. 'Hi, Mr Odd!'

Odd Martin, walking with green paper dollars in his fingers, counted them. He stopped on one spot and held himself in one position. His eyes were senseless.

'Radney,' he cried out. 'Radney!' His hands groped.

'Yes, sir, Mr Odd!'

'Radney, where was I going? Just now, where was I going? Going somewhere to buy something for Miss Weldon! Here, Radney, help me!'

'Yes, sir, Mr Odd!' Radney ran and stood in his shadow.

A hand came down, money in it, seventy dollars of money. 'Radney, run buy a dress for – Miss Weldon –' The hand opened, the money fell, the hand remained out, opening, making grasping, seeking moves, wrestling, wondering moves. There was numbed terror and longing and fear in Odd's face. 'The place, I can't remember the place, oh God, help me remember. A dress, and a coat. For Miss Weldon, at – at –'

'Krausmann's Department Store?' said Radney.

'No.'

'Fielder's?'

'No!'

'Mr Leiberman's?'

'That's it! Leiberman! Here, here, Radney, run down to –'

'Leiberman's.'

'– and get a new green dress for – Miss Weldon, and a coat. A new green dress with yellow roses painted on it. You get them and bring them to me here. Oh, Radney, wait.'

'Yes, sir?'

'Radney – you think, maybe, I could clean up at your house?' asked Odd quietly. 'I need a – a bath.'

'Gee, I don't know, Mr Odd. My folks're funny. I don't know.'

'That's all right, Radney. I understand. Run now!'

Radney ran on the double. Odd Martin stood in the sunlight, humming a tune in his mouth. Radney ran with the money past the barber shop; poked his head inside. Mr Simpson stopped snipping Mr Trumbull's hair and glared at him.

'Hey!' cried Radney. 'Odd Martin's humming a tune!'

'What tune?' asked Simpson.

'Goes like *this*,' and Radney hummed it.

'Ye God's Amaughty!' bellowed Simpson. 'So *that*'s why Miss Weldon ain't here manicurin' this mornin'! That there tune's the Weddin' March!'

Radney rushed on. Pandemonium!

Shouting, laughter, a squishing and pattering of water. The back room of the barber emporium steamed and sweated. Everybody had his turn. Mr Simpson heaved a bucket of hot water down over Odd Martin sitting in a galvanized tin tub. Mr Trumbull banged and whisked Odd's pale back with a big beardy brush on a stick. Old man Gilpatrick doused him with a half quart of cow-soap, that bubbled and frothed and stank sweetly, and every once in a while Shorty Phillips hit Odd with a jigger of eau de cologne. They all funned and ran around, slipping, in the steam. 'Put some more on 'em!' More water. 'Scrub with that brush, *you*!' The brush sizzled on Odd's spine. Mr Simpson gunked in his throat, laughing: 'Always said marriage is what you needed, Odd!' Somebody else said, 'Congratulations!' and smacked Odd right square on his shoulder blades with a can of ice-water. Odd Martin didn't even notice the shock. 'You'll smell fine now!'

Odd sat blowing bubbles in one cupped hand. 'Thanks. Thanks so much for helping. Thanks for scouring me. Thanks. I needed it.'

Simpson put a hand over his own smiling mouth. 'Nothing's too good for you, ya know that, Odd.'

Someone whispered in the steamy background, 'Imagine . . . her . . . him . . . and married . . . moron married . . . to an idiot . . . why . . .'

'Shut up, back there!' Simpson frowned.

Radney ran in. 'Here's the green dress, Mr Odd!'

An hour later they perched Odd in the barber chair. Someone had lent him a new pair of black shoes. Mr Trumbull polished them vigorously, winking at everybody. Mr Simpson snipped Odd's hair, took no money for it. 'No, Odd, keep your money. This is all a weddin' present to you. Yes, sir.' And he spat. Then he shook rose-water on Odd's scalp. 'There, moonlight and roses!'

Odd Martin looked around. 'You won't tell nobody about this marriage,' he asked, 'until tomorrow? Me and Miss Weldon sort of want a marriage without the town poking fun. You see?'

'Sure, Odd,' said Simpson, finishing the job. 'Mum's the word. Where you goin' to live? You buyin' a farm?'

'Farm?' Odd stepped from the chair. Somebody'd lent him a nice new tan coat, and someone else'd pressed his pants sharp for him. He looked elegant. 'Yes, I'm going over to buy the property now. Have to pay extra, but it's worth it. Extra. Come on, Radney.' He paused at the door. 'I bought a house out on the edge of town. I have to go make the payment on it now.'

Simpson stopped him. 'What's it like? You didn't have much money.'

'It's a small house,' said Odd, 'but it'll do. Some folks built it a while back, then moved away East somewhere. It was up for sale for only five hundred, so I got it. Miss Weldon and I are moving out there tonight, after our marriage. But don't tell nobody, please, until tomorrow.'

'Sure thing, Odd. Sure thing.'

Odd went away into the four o'clock light, Radney at his side, and the barber shop men fell down into chairs and grabbed their ribs and laughed.

The sun went down slow and the snipping of the shears continued, with the buzzing of flies, the clock ticking, and the men sitting around nodding their heads, showing their teeth, waving their hands, joking . . .

The next morning at breakfast, little Radney Bellows sat thoughtfully spooning his cereal. Father folded his newspaper across the table and looked at Mother. 'Everybody in town's talking about the quiet elopement of Odd Martin and Miss Weldon,' said Father. 'People, looking for them, can't find them.'

'Well,' said Mother, 'I heard he bought her a house.'

'I heard that, too,' admitted Father. 'I phoned Carl Rogers this morning. He says he didn't sell any house to Odd. And Carl is the only real-estate dealer in town.'

Radney Bellows swallowed more cereal. He looked at his father. 'Oh, no, he's not the *only* real-estate dealer in town.'

'What do you mean?' demanded Father.

'Nothing, except I looked out the window at midnight and I saw something.'

'You saw *what*?'

'It was all moonlight. And you know what I saw? Well, I saw two people walking up the Elm Glade road. A man and a woman. A man in a nice new coat, and a woman in a green dress. Walking real slow. Holding hands.' Radney took a breath. 'And the two people were Mr Odd Martin and Miss Weldon. And walking out the Elm Glade road there ain't any houses out that way at all. Only the Trinity Park Cemetery. And Mr Gustavsson, in town, he sells tombs in the Trinity Park Cemetery. He's got an office in town. Like I said, Mr Carl Rogers ain't the only real-estate man in town. So –'

'Oh,' snorted Father, irritably, 'you were dreaming!'

Radney bent his head over his cereal and looked out from the corners of his eyes.

'Yes, sir,' he said finally, sighing. 'I was only dreaming.'